Sadie's GUARDED HARBOR

DANIELLE M HAAS

This is a work of fiction. Names, characters, places, and incidents are the product of the author's imagination or are used fictitiously , and any resemblance to actual persons, living or dead, business establishments, events or locals is entirely coincidental.

Cover created by Deranged Doctor Designs.

A Danielle M Haas Publishing Book

Sadie's Guarded Harbor - Safe Haven Women's Shelter

To my kind and loving Abigail. Always be strong, always be brave, and always be you.

A NOTE TO THE READER

To my wonderful reader,

Thank you so much for choosing to read Sadie's Guarded Refuge. Before you begin, I wanted to let you know this book contains themes of domestic abuse.

If you or anyone you know finds yourself in an abusive situation and you need someone to talk to, please call the National Domestic Violence Hotline at 1-800-799-SAFE (1-800-799-7233).

1

"Mommy! Turn off the ceiling lights!"

Sadie Pennel couldn't help but smile at the excitement pouring off her daughter in waves as she hung the last ornament on the Christmas tree. A heady warmth burrowed into her chest, and she fought the urge to pull Amelia into a hug before shutting off the living room lights at Safe Haven Women's Shelter.

Not like her rambunctious six-year-old would stop for one second and let her mama get in a quick cuddle.

"What do you say?" she asked, hovering her hand above the switch.

Mrs. Collins, the owner of the shelter, chuckled. She'd hung her wire-framed glasses around her neck with a bright red chain and situated a Santa hat on the side of her head at a jaunty angle. "She's shaking like a tick on a dog's tail. She just might explode if you don't get them living room lights off so we can see this Christmas tree in all its lit-up glory."

Amelia giggled and bounced on her toes. Her dirty blond pigtails swayed with the motion. "I'm not a tick."

Sadie rolled her eyes and grinned. Over the past year, she and her daughter had spent countless hours at the shelter, volunteering their time and talents to help women and children in need. Amelia had wrapped the people they'd come to call family around her finger in no time. "Tick or no tick, I still need a please."

"Please, Mama." Amelia pressed her hands into a prayer pose under her chin.

Another shelter volunteer, Marie Robinson, stood beside the tree with her squirming baby on her hip and the plug for the Christmas tree in her free hand. "You better hurry. Even Nora's getting anxious."

"Fine, fine." Sadie flipped down the switch, drowning the room in darkness for a few seconds before colorful twinkly lights bathed the room in a warm glow.

Sadie smiled, a peace she'd searched for her entire youth nestling over her shoulders like a warm blanket. Green garland was wrapped over the stair railing with big red bows and homemade paper snowflakes hung from the ceiling in front of the built-in bookshelves. Red and white knit stockings waited to be filled above the fireplace, the flickering flames adding to the festive ambiance.

Amelia squealed and ran to Sadie, wrapping her arms around her. "So pretty!"

Sadie smoothed her palm down Amelia's back and fought tears prickling the corners of her eyes. Most people took moments like this for granted, but not her. She'd grown up bouncing from run-down homes and sketchy houses to countless shelters as her mother struggled to stop the cycle of abuse she'd been caught in most her life.

Things like tree lightings and quiet evenings with hot cocoa and a roaring fire hadn't existed. She'd been lucky to go to bed on Christmas night—or any night for that matter—with a full stomach. When she'd gotten pregnant with her own daughter, Sadie had vowed to give her more. To be more.

And now, she was determined to teach her daughter they had an obligation to show kindness and compassion to others. To help mothers and their children the same way people had stepped in to help her and her mother so long ago.

Marie snuggled her baby close and sighed. "You're right, Amelia. This is the most beautiful Christmas tree I've ever seen."

Sadie understood the catch in Marie's voice. Only months before, Marie had stayed at the shelter as a mother in trouble. Now she was a woman in love with a bright future ahead. She had brought a whole new path for support to the shelter and given Amelia another surrogate sister to dote on, which delighted her to no end.

"Nora's first Christmas will be a great one." Mrs. Collins stroked the chubby baby's cheek then squeezed Marie's hand. "And so will every other one that follows."

Sadie wanted nothing more than to stay in this moment and soak up the positive vibes, but she had a room to ready for a woman arriving in an hour. "Glad we got this done and we can give everyone something cheerful to enjoy. This time of year is even harder to take that first step away from a tough situation. Amelia, be a good girl while I run upstairs and make sure we have everything in place."

"Mrs. Collins said we could bake cookies. Can we do that now? Please?" She drew out the last word into a cheerful whine only an excited child could pull off.

"It's getting late, honey. Close to bedtime. We'll have to head home soon."

Amelia's face fell. "I want to stay here."

The sentiment was one Sadie heard every time they had to leave the shelter and head back to Water's Edge. Their small town was only a fifteen-minute drive from where the shelter was located in Pine Valley, Tennessee, but Amelia often acted as though their house was on another planet. After spending so much time in Pine Valley, Sadie had considered moving to the place that now felt like home.

But she liked having some distance between where she worked and the place she could fully be herself and let down her walls. Focus solely on her daughter and the people at the shelter who depended on her.

"Knock, knock. I come bearing gifts."

The sound of her fellow deputy's voice chased away all the happiness glowing inside Sadie. Tommy Wells stood in the doorway in his wrinkle-free uniform and a sack of goodies dangling over his shoulder. Snowflakes dampened his brown hair and his charming smile made dimples flash on his cheeks.

If she didn't find him so irritating, the combination of wholesome officer of the law and pretend jolly toy maker would be endearing. Instead, her guard instantly went up. Tommy represented all the carefree, flirty men who used whatever they had at their disposal to get ahead in life.

Just like all the men who used her mother then left her behind when she was no longer needed.

No, sheriff's deputy or not, Tommy Wells was a man she couldn't trust. And she planned to stay as far away from him as possible.

Tommy stomped his boots on the front mat in the foyer before stepping into the living room and admiring the transformation from a cozy spot to a magical wonderland. He loved this time of year. Loved even more that he could do his part in bringing just the tiniest piece of joy to anyone who used the old Victorian house as a stopping point on their road to a better place.

"Unk! Unk!" Nora kicked her legs and reached for him.

Amelia giggled. "I think she's talking."

He grinned at Sadie's adorable daughter. Her freckled face was just like her mother's but always so much friendlier. Her wide smile showcased her missing front tooth, where Sadie's constant scowl broadcast her disdain and kept him at arm's length.

"She's saying uncle. I'm her favorite person, ya know." He shot Amelia a wink then nodded at Sadie and Mrs. Collins before grinning at Marie. "I'll trade you the bag for the baby."

"She's so heavy these days, I'll take any chance to offload her on someone else." Marie handed over the happy baby and grabbed the bag, untying the top to peek inside. "Holy moly, this is so generous. Where did all these gifts come from?"

Tommy shrugged. "Just took what my sister gave me. I'm only the delivery man."

Sadie coughed to cover a strangled sound.

He faced her, head tilted to the side and brows raised high. "You doing okay over there?"

She straightened and stared him dead in the eyes. "Something went down the wrong way, that's all."

"I'll get you water, Mama." Amelia raced out of the room, the echo of her hurried footsteps lingering even after she disappeared.

"I better go help before she makes a mess." Sadie offered a tight smile before following her daughter.

Marie chuckled, drawing her attention to him.

"What?" he asked.

Mrs. Collins clicked her tongue. "You always stick in that girl's craw."

"Not sure why. I hardly speak with her, but I'm not wasting time on it. Not when I have this little cutie to focus on. Look at those curls, Nora." He tugged at the end of a dark lock and the baby giggled. "My brother's going to have his hands full when you get older. Good thing you'll have both of us to watch out for you."

"Poor kid won't stand a chance. Maybe once you have a family of your own my little lady will get more breathing room." Marie swept Nora back into her arms and pressed a kiss to her cheek.

His arms were suddenly as empty as his heart. The day his brother Owen had fallen for Marie and Nora, he'd gotten a glimpse of the family he'd never have. He adored his niece—and the nephew his sister had given him—but his future didn't hold the same cards for him.

Not after ripping away the only two women he'd ever loved, leaving him to live a life that would never be entirely whole.

Amelia dashed back into the room with Sadie on her heels. She stopped right in front of him and grinned with both hands behind her back. "I got something for ya."

"Oh really." He crouched low to meet the little girl on her level and ignored the hard stare heating the side of his face from her mother.

Amelia gave one big nod. "Yep. But ya gotta guess a hand."

He tapped the tip of his finger against his chin. "Hmm, the right hand."

She swished her lips to the side as if trying to figure out her left from her right then presented the correct one, palm outstretched. A green tin foil wrapped candy greeted him.

"For me?" He pressed a hand to his chest and gasped.

"Uh huh. Merry Christmas, Mr. Tommy."

He swiped the chocolate, unwrapping it quickly and popping it in his mouth. "Thank you. Best treat ever."

If Sadie wasn't hovering over them like she was about to smack him upside the head, he'd give the little girl a hug. But no way he'd poke that bear.

Standing, he pulled lightly on one of Amelia's pigtails. "All right ladies. I've made my delivery and now it's time to head to work."

Sadie frowned. "You're working an overnight shift?"

The drip of disbelief in her voice raised his hackles. He tensed the muscles in his neck to keep from reacting, something he had to do far too often due to his father's position as the county sheriff. Most people assumed he'd been handed his job, but they couldn't be further from the truth.

Not many people realized he had to put in more hours and work ten times harder to get an ounce of respect. That fact might be a tough pill to swallow, but he'd do it every damn day to get where he wanted.

"Yep. I'm covering a shift. Don't mind helping when needed." He wouldn't give her any more information. Her prickly attitude had kept him away from the minute she'd moved into town, and there was no reason to try being more than coworkers. Thank God their paths didn't often cross even at work.

Hell, he saw her more at the shelter than he ever did around town in Water's Edge. He just hoped she gave the women who came here a little more friendliness than she passed around the station.

"Can I send you out on the roads with more than a chocolate?" Mrs. Collins asked, breaking into the tension cracking between him and Sadie.

Shoving his feelings about Sadie to the side, he focused on the petite gray-haired woman in the red velvet jumper who reminded him so much of the grandmother he missed. "Nah. I'm fine. Thanks, though. Y'all have a good evening."

He gave his soon-to-be sister-in-law a side hug and kissed Nora's forehead. "You two drive safe when you head home. The roads are a little icy."

"We'll be safe, but I'll call Owen if I need to," Marie said.

He waved at Mrs. Collins then dipped his chin at Sadie. "Same to you. Supposed to get more snow tonight."

Sadie pressed her lips into a flat line. "I'll be fine."

He swallowed back a snort. He might not care if Sadie knew what a pain in the ass he found her to be, but he had too much respect for everyone else in the room to show it. Keeping his smile in place he gave a little wave and walked back out to the frigid air, leaving the ice queen behind him.

2

Frigid air bit into Sadie turned-up nose. She didn't mind. The brutal wind barreled into her and woke her mind. Not everything she'd done in the military stuck with her after leaving the service, but an early morning run to start the day was something she'd never give up.

No matter how cold.

Shaking out her limbs, she started along the same path she took daily. Down the country road to the rough trail in the patch of woods a mile from her house. She didn't have much time this morning after taking Amelia to spend the day with Mrs. Collins, but she could get a couple miles in before hitting the shower and heading to work.

Turning from the road, she increased her pace and headed into the cover of thick trees. Wisps of her chestnut hair slipped from the rubber band and whipped against her face. The branches were bare this time of year, but the mangle of limbs still stretched overhead and blocked most of the glow of the sun shimmering just above the horizon.

The worn path narrowed, the skinny trees almost taking over the trail. She lifted her arm to block the twisted limbs. A few more steps and the path would widen before reaching the clearing. If she pushed herself a little bit harder, she'd make it in time to see the sun coming over the peaks of the Smoky Mountains. Then she could rest her lungs for a beat and bask in the glorious new day.

She pounded forward, huffing out the cold air in spirals. The trees pushed apart, making more space as she moved seamlessly toward the clearing. The break in the foliage came into view. Sadie slowed her pace and stepped up to the tree line. Leaning forward, she rested her arms on her knees and drew in a few deep breaths. Her heart pounded against her rib cage.

Standing tall, she placed her open palms on the back of her head. She lifted her gaze to the sky and warmth bloomed in her despite the chilly air. Vibrant splashes of color blossomed, the sun casting its glow on the crisp December day. A slight dusting of snow scattered along the field. Three black birds hovered in the sky, one after the other swooping low and cawing, the noise echoing through the silent sky.

A mound of green poking through the fresh white snow caught her attention. Nothing of that color should be littering the meadow. She took another step forward, straining to make out what lingered in the field.

Intuition tingled the base of her neck. She stepped slowly, keeping on high-alert while grabbing her cell phone from the side pocket of her yoga pants. The closer she got, the more the dread in the pit of her stomach grew. The birds screamed their call, warning her away, but she had to know—had to see what they'd found.

Coming to a stop, she covered her mouth with her hand and pressed the contact button for the sheriff's station. Glassy eyes stared up at her. A dead man, skin frozen, gunshot wound in the center of his forehead.

"Millerton County Sheriff's Station."

The deputy on the desk's voice sounded distant against the growing alarm in her mind. She pulled herself together, scanning the area for signs that anyone still lingered. "This is Deputy Pennel. I need assistance in the meadow off Graham Road. I just found Shawn Downs."

A harsh laugh sounded on the line. "He passed out in a field this time, huh? At least he didn't get himself into any trouble."

Sadie cleared her throat, breaking up the shock and emotion lodge inside. "He didn't pass out. He's dead. Someone killed him."

A YAWN STRETCHED Tommy's mouth as he stepped out of his cruiser, parked on the side of the road, and stomped through the tall, brittle grass. Wind whipped against him with no barriers to keep it at bay. He shoved his hands into the pockets of his jacket, keeping his head bent down and feet moving. He was only an hour from being off-shift. All he wanted was to go home, curl into a warm bed, and sleep for the next twelve hours.

From the sound of the call from dispatch, that dream wouldn't be a reality for longer than he cared to admit.

Trudging toward the center of the meadow, he lifted a hand in greeting to Deputy Pennel. "Morning. Dispatch says you think you found Shawn Downs—dead."

She offered a tight smile and dipped her chin. "I don't think. I know."

Sadie wouldn't have said a name if she hadn't been certain. The woman was thorough as hell, but he couldn't help pushing her buttons. "How can you be sure he's dead? Hope you didn't contaminate the scene." He shrugged, stopping at the feet of the victim.

"The bullet between his eyes was a pretty good indication." She crossed her arms over her chest.

Tommy glanced down and cringed. "Shit."

"And I didn't contaminate a damn thing. I'm not an idiot. I wasn't prepared for a crime scene, so no way I'd touch or move anything."

Slipping his backpack from his shoulders, he unzipped the bag and pulled out two pairs of gloves, tossing a pair toward Sadie. "Might as well help me while you're here."

Sadie snorted and slipped the gloves on her hands.

"What brought you out to the middle of nowhere at sunrise?" He cast her a quick glance and tried not to stare too long at the adorable freckles that dominated her face.

"I always run in the woods before my shift. I stopped to admire the sunrise and noted birds swooping down. I wanted to know what they'd found." A shiver had her hands dancing up and down the thin long sleeves covering her arms.

"How long have you been out here? You must be freezing." Hating his sense of chivalry, he took off his coat and extended it toward her. "Take it."

"I'm fine. I haven't been outside too long." She rose her pert nose in the air. "Let's secure the scene."

Biting back a groan of frustration, he shrugged back into his jacket. If she wanted to freeze, so be it. He tried to be nice every time he saw her, but she preferred to be a pain in the ass.

He grabbed yellow crime scene tape from his bag and handed it to her. "Have at it." Establishing a perimeter wouldn't be a fun task, so he'd let her deal with the logistics. He'd study the scene and make a call to the coroner.

Sadie stomped away, and Tommy crouched in front of Shawn. A red hole marked the middle of his forehead. A pool of blood lay on the other side, next to Shawn's shoulder, and Tommy gently moved the body for a better view. Another gunshot wound penetrated the shoulder blade. Queasiness took over his stomach. Logic told him Shawn was shot from behind first, then took a bullet to the head.

Sadie came back as he finished his examination. "Looks like he was shot execution style, like you used to see in the military. Handgun most likely."

Tommy rose and studied Sadie's wide green eyes as they stayed locked on Shawn. "Why would someone shoot him from behind then come close range for another shot?"

Sadie lifted her gaze to his. "To make sure Shawn knew who wanted him dead."

The truth of her words made him shudder. It would have been easy to make Shawn's death look like an accident. Shawn often hunted with friends and was drunk more than he wasn't. But whoever killed Shawn cared more about making himself known to his victim than setting a stage to help get away with murder.

The shrill ring of his phone cut through the silence. A quick glance at the screen announced his dad as the caller. Tommy shouldn't be surprised. As the county sheriff, Mike Wells knew everything that happened in his jurisdiction. And news of Shawn's death would have reached him at warp speed. Answering the call, he brought the phone to his ear. "Hey, Dad."

"I hear you were called to the scene for the suspected death of Shawn Downs. What are we looking at?"

"Murder."

"Sonofabitch."

Tommy kicked a snow drift with the tip of his boot. "Tell me about it."

"I know we're short staffed, but I want you and Deputy Pennel working on this together." The order came out in a tone Tommy knew too well—one that warned not to argue.

Too damn bad.

He turned away from Sadie, taking a few steps in the opposite direction so his voice wouldn't carry on the howling breeze. "You've got to be kidding. I don't need a partner. I was called to the scene. I'll handle it."

"We need two people on this. This isn't some petty theft case you can track down in a day. It's a murder. We need all hands on deck, and those hands will be yours and Deputy Pennel's. Do you understand me?"

"Yes, sir." He ground out the words through clenched teeth and disconnected the call. Pivoting, he faced Sadie.

Her eyes bored into his, questions clear as the morning sky.

He fought to keep his gaze on the hints of yellow in her green irises and not the way her tight running clothes molded against her toned body.

He shoved a hand through his too-long hair and made his way to her. She wouldn't like what he was about to say any more than he did. As he approached her, one thought circled in his mind. They needed to find Shawn Downs' killer fast because spending too much time with the constantly uptight Sadie Pennel just might be the death of him.

3

Frustration simmered in Sadie's bones. She might not have been on shift when she'd stumbled upon the death scene, but that was no reason not to make her the deputy in charge.

The only deputy.

She kept her narrowed gaze locked on the Millerton County Logo dominating the back of Tommy's jacket as he spoke with the coroner by the now-loaded van. Just her luck the sheriff's son was called to the scene. The last person on the force she'd want to be stuck with.

A gust of wind swept over her. She should have at least taken his coat when she'd had the chance. But dammit, she didn't want anything handed to her—even if her own pride was now the reason she couldn't feel her arms anymore.

Tommy broke away from the white-haired man by the road and stomped toward her with his mouth set in a grim line. She studied the angles of his face, the rough edges softened by the deep dimples that usually accompanied his almost constant smile. His happy-go-lucky attitude grated on her nerves with every encounter they had. Proof, in her mind, life had gone easy on him.

She tore away her gaze and followed the barely visible tracks in the still-falling snow. Wasting time being bitter about Tommy Wells' perfect life wouldn't get her anywhere and wouldn't do anything to soften the blows of her own past. She needed to do what she always did—keep her mind on-task and focus on the job. Prove her worth. Advance through hard work and dedication.

She cast a quick glance over her shoulder, hating the flutter in the pit of her stomach as Tommy came closer. No, spending any amount of time thinking about Tommy would lead to nothing but trouble.

"Talked to Doc. The coroner's office is swamped, but he'll try to get Shawn's autopsy done as quick as possible. Getting the details on the gun used to kill him could be critical." Tommy shoved his hands in his pocket and dropped his gaze to the imprint of Shawn's body on the crumpled grass.

Sadie made an exaggerated show of glancing at her watch. "Your shift's over. I can take it from here."

"We both know that won't happen. Not when the order to work together came from the sheriff."

"You mean your dad." Mumbling under her breath, she spun toward the tree line, tracking the fading footprints. Life had handed her a deadbeat dad who'd taken off before she'd said her first word, had taken Amelia's own father from them before her daughter had even been born. Knowing Tommy had probably been handed his job on a shiny platter by his father scratched at the constant bitterness always trying to break through the surface.

"Excuse me?" Tommy quickened his pace to match hers.

"Nothing." She stopped, crouching low to study the thin blanket of snow. "Two sets of tracks. Treads are different, but the size is similar. Male, most likely. Did Shawn have any known enemies?"

Tommy shook his head. "The guy was a harmless drunk. Never hurt anyone. Kept mostly to himself."

She rose to her full height, which at five foot six was a full head shorter than Tommy. "Any idea why he'd be out here last night?" If she was forced to work with Tommy, she had to make sure he saw her as a leader. Though it probably wouldn't be long before he tossed his weight—and name—around to get things done his way.

Tommy shrugged. "He liked to hunt with his buddies. But I don't see a rifle. Could have dropped it if he was running."

"Then let's check the woods." She made her way toward the trees, close to the path she abandoned when she'd found Shawn's body. She kept her gaze to the ground, searching for anything out of the ordinary.

Tommy stayed by her side. "I heard what you said."

Her spine went rigid, but she didn't respond.

"You think my dad pulled strings to get me on the case, don't you?" A hint of laughter laced through his voice.

She stopped and studied him. A faint smile curved his wide mouth but a hardness in his hazel eyes told a different story. A hundred words about nepotism and laughing your way through life danced on the tip of her tongue, but she held them back. Her opinion about how Tommy landed his job and the helping hand he got along the way wouldn't change anything.

"What I think doesn't matter." She stepped forward, but a hand on her arm stopped her.

"It matters to me." Tommy's unflinching scrutiny made her hesitate.

Shivering, she yanked away. "My opinion shouldn't matter."

Pivoting, Tommy blocked her path. "You don't like me. Fine. I'm not too fond of you either. But we're stuck together until this is over. Might as well play nice."

She pressed her lips together and made sure not to stop and admire the broad set of his shoulders. "Fine." If nothing else, the Army taught her how to keep her mouth shut and get along with people she didn't like. Wasn't that a lesson she tried to teach Amelia? You don't always have to like everyone, but you have to be kind—or in this case, civil.

She could put up with Tommy until this mess was settled. Besides, this was the type of case that could get her the recognition she'd worked so damn hard for—that sent her up the ladder in a station filled with men who often looked down their fat noses at her.

A glint of silver caught her eye. She sidestepped Tommy and hurried toward it. The familiar logo of a beer company, covered in icy crystals, winked in the sun. "Looks like Shawn was drinking last night."

The crunching of mangled leaves and snow announced Tommy's approach. "Shawn was always drinking, but the autopsy will confirm it." He grabbed a clear evidence bag from his backpack and collected the can. "We'll check for prints. He might have had a drinking buddy last night."

Sadie dipped her chin toward a tree stand nestled in the trees, the thickening snow now concealing anything from the night before. "Let's check out the stand. Maybe something else was left behind."

They moved in silence. She might have agreed to play nice, but the truce did nothing to quell the tension pulsing between them. She made it to the ladder first and climbed to the top. Wide wooden planks made up the floor, a split railing along the perimeter.

Nothing.

She walked slowly around the square structure. Tommy's shoulder brushed against her in the small space. Her foot crunched a patch of ice, and she dropped to a squat. The yellowish hue told her the ice wasn't made from water.

Leaning forward, she sniffed. "Beer. Someone was up here drinking."

Standing, she studied the surrounding area. They sat in the middle of a dense patch of woods with the wide-open meadow twenty feet to one side. She pictured what was outside the woods in her mind's eye. "Either someone came with Shawn to have a drink in the freezing woods then shot him, or someone followed him here."

Tommy stood beside her. "I bet the latter."

Her gut said the same, but she was curious to his reasoning. "What makes you think that?"

"Shawn was shot in the back, as if he was running away from someone. Someone close enough to share a beer could just shoot him and be done."

"I agree."

Tommy widened his eyes and smacked a hand over his heart. "I didn't know that was possible."

She couldn't help the laugh that broke loose from her pursed lips. "I always agree with logic. Don't get used to it."

He grinned, the dimples on his cheeks deepening. "Are you saying I'm not usually logical?"

She shrugged, turning away. The charm that oozed from him threatened to suck her under his spell. She couldn't let that happen. Not when getting wrapped up with someone like Tommy Wells could threaten everything she'd worked so hard for—threaten her very reputation. "I wouldn't know."

"That's right. You barely know me but have decided not to like me. Why is that?"

Sadie ran a hand over her ponytail and made her way to the ladder. She cast a glance in his direction before descending. "We have bigger issues to worry about than why I refuse to fall at your feet. I'm more concerned with finding who killed Shawn. But first, we need to visit next of kin and let them know Shawn was murdered."

All humor left his face, the grim expression from before returning.

For a second, she wished for the carefree smile to come back, the charm to pour through him and threaten to intoxicate her. Ignoring Tommy was much easier when she could tell herself he was just another man-child taking handouts and skating through life. This other side of Tommy shook her more than she cared to admit. It told her he was a man hellbent on cracking a case.

And it was sexy as hell.

~

AFTER TAKING a quick pit stop by Sadie's place so she could change into her uniform, Tommy stood beside her on the large stoop in front of the giant brick-colonial house in the center of town. He'd much rather be back at her cozy house in the woods. Surrounded by framed photos of Amelia and her artwork stuck to the fridge.

But anywhere was better than here.

Wiping his sweaty palm on the thigh of his trousers, he cast a quick glance at Sadie. "Ready?"

She nodded, lips pressed together and focus trained on the cherry-stained wood door.

"Here we go." Tommy rang the doorbell then clasped his hands in front of him.

The steady thump of distant footsteps came closer, and the door swung wide. A scowl set on the petite face of Judge Melissa Downs, her crisp black suit framing her slender body. The scowl transformed into a confused smile. "Hello, there Tommy. Deputy Pennel. Can I help you with something?"

Sadie stiffened beside him, probably at the sound of his first name spoken so casually from the county judge. But he couldn't let her reaction to something he had no control over affect him. "Good morning, ma'am. Could we step in for a minute?"

"Please, call me Melissa." She straightened the white collar under her jacket and blocked the entrance, turning down the request to come inside. "I've got to leave soon for church. Either make it quick, or you'll have to come back."

"We need to speak with you about your husband," Sadie said. "We regret to inform you Shawn was found dead this morning."

Melissa dropped her hand, and all the color left her tanned face. Her bright blue eyes bore into Sadie. "Excuse me?"

Tommy fisted his hands at his sides. He hadn't considered asking her to have a bit more compassion—a bit more respect—when delivering the death of someone's loved one. It was no secret around town Shawn and Melissa had been estranged for years, the reason they'd never officially divorced a source of constant gossip and rumors. But that didn't mean she didn't care for Shawn or should be denied an ounce of kindness.

He forced the muscles in his face to convey empathy and not annoyance. "I'm so sorry, but it's true. Deputy Pennel discovered Shawn this morning outside of town. Can we come in and speak with you for a moment?"

Melissa stumbled backward, bracing herself with a trembling hand on a small table tucked along the wall behind the door. "I can't...I mean...are you sure? It can't be Shawn. There has to be a mistake."

"No mistake," Tommy said, fighting to keep his voice steady. He hadn't necessarily been friends with Shawn, but he'd known the guy most of his life. Hell, he stopped by the bar Shawn worked at a couple times a week to keep abreast of what was happening in the community.

More times than not, he offered a helping hand to Shawn—a ride to an AA meeting, a listening ear. Not that Shawn ever took it. And now he'd never get the chance to put his life on the right path.

"We're very sorry for your loss. We're determined to find the person responsible for Shawn's death. We need to ask you a few questions." Sadie placed emphasis on the last few words, clearly agitated that Melissa refused to let them inside.

Melissa's posture snapped up straight, grief making ripples along her forehead. "What do you mean? Someone killed him?"

Tommy ground together his teeth. Sadie had as much tact as a toddler. "Yes."

"I need to see him. Now." Melissa swiped a pair of keys from on top of the table and gripped the edge of the door. "Where is he? The morgue?"

Tommy nodded.

"I'll answer whatever questions you have later. Right now, I need to see my husband." The door slammed shut.

Tucking his chin, Tommy jammed his hands in his jacket pockets and headed for his car. His blood pumped furiously, making the frigid December weather feel like summer. Out of all the ways he'd envisioned this conversation going, never had he thought Sadie would be such an ass. Sure, they should have discussed how they'd break the news, but what the hell was she thinking?

Yanking open the door, he settled into the driver's seat and turned over the engine. Heat flooded through the vents, and he shut it off. He needed to cool down. He kept his gaze trained ahead, not wanting to watch Sadie as she made her way to the car.

The passenger door opened, and Sadie sat ram-rod straight in the seat. She turned a hard glare his way. "What's your problem?"

Tommy stared slack-jawed at her pursed lips. "My problem? Are you kidding me? You walked up and dropped a bomb on that woman, changing everything in her life, without an ounce of sympathy."

She closed her eyes on a long blink, her body rigid, before settling her glassy eyes on him. "Have you ever told someone they've lost a loved one before? Ever been told someone you loved has died? I've lived through both. Trust me, pulling off the band-aid is a lot easier when you just rip the damn thing off."

Her admission stole the words of condemnation from his tongue. He'd never had an actual conversation with Sadie, had no clue what her life was like before she moved to Water's Edge. Swallowing his anger, he opted for a different approach. "I've never had to deliver this kind of news before, and I'm sorry you've lived through it. Nothing would make it easier for someone to hear. That, I do know from experience."

The muscles in Sadie's face didn't relax, but a hint of surprise sharpened her eyes. "You do?"

He nodded. "My mother. I'm used to everyone in town knowing my business. Sometimes I forget you didn't grow up here."

She settled back into the seat and dropped her gaze to her lap. "I'm sorry. I understand how hard it is to lose someone you love."

Tommy folded his hands around the steering wheel to keep from reaching out and placing a hand on her arm, her knee—hell anywhere to show her how sorry he was for her loss. Something told him she wouldn't appreciate the gesture. "I'm sorry, too. Losing someone you love sucks."

Sadie let out a long sigh. "Sure does. What happened to your mom?"

The muscles in his heart pinched together. His mom might have died years ago, but it didn't lessen the pain. "Hit and run. Some bastard mowed her down when she was walking on the sidewalk and drove away like she wasn't worth their time. Never caught who did it."

"Unresolved wounds are the hardest to heal."

Something in her voice made him take a closer look at the slight dip of her full lips. The hint of lingering sadness in her green eyes. "Do you have unresolved wounds?"

She set her mouth back in a tight line and turned to stare out the window. "My wounds don't matter. All that matters is finding a killer before he strikes again."

He'd been wrong. Sadie Pennel wasn't unsympathetic and full of pointy edges. She carried around her own demons. Demons she worked damn hard to keep hidden beneath a tough shell.

His conscience itched to ask more questions, but instead he pulled onto the quiet street. They had a list of people to talk to. He didn't need to waste energy wondering about a woman who'd never open up to him. His job demanded his attention, and Shawn Downs demanded justice.

4

Tommy stepped over the threshold into Shawn's trailer. Empty beer cans scattered through the limited space. The stench of stale, rotten trash permeated the wood-laminate walls. Tommy wrinkled his nose and moved further inside, making room for Sadie.

"How in the world can people live like this?" Sadie skirted around him, kicking discarded cans from her path. She left the door open a crack, allowing the cool breeze to billow in and help with the odor.

"Shawn didn't give a rat's ass about much besides drinking. I'm not surprised to find the place such a mess." Tommy roamed his gaze from one corner of the space to the next. A stain-covered tan sofa lined the narrow living room, and a single chair sat with its back to the cramped kitchen, facing the television.

"It's sad." Sadie stepped lightly into the kitchen, taking care not to smash the aluminum cans. "Seems like the guy came from a good family. Probably had every opportunity to make something of his life. How did he end up here? Did you know him?" She opened the cabinets with her glove-covered hands.

Tommy sighed, more depressed than he anticipated by Shawn's living quarters. Sadie was right. Shawn had every chance to do something—anything—with his life. But he'd wasted it on alcohol. "I always knew *of* him. He's quite a few years older than me. I've tried recently to help the guy out, but he wasn't much of a talker. But it's a small town. Everyone knows everyone. Especially Shawn."

Sadie dropped her hand to her side and glared at him with narrowed eyes. "What does that mean?"

Tommy yanked out a pair of gloves from his pocket and stuffed his hands in them. He wasn't sure what they'd find in this mess, but he wanted to do the job quickly and get the hell out of here. "He was very different when he was younger. All-star athlete. Good student. His dad was a big-shot lawyer for years."

"Do you think there was more going on than people realized? A seedy secret or pastime he kept under the radar? I mean, how does a kid with everything end with this?" Turning her palm upward, she extended her arm to indicate the gloomy space.

"His mom died while he was away at school. That might have messed with him—not being around when she was dying." Tommy's mother's death clung to him like the plague. He could understand how tragically losing someone close could eat away at you to the point where you turned to the comfort of booze.

Hell, Tommy's mother's death wasn't the only one that tortured him. Losing Vanessa had been just as brutal and difficult to deal with. A familiar ache intensified in his chest, and he rubbed a hand over his sternum. He couldn't let himself go down that rabbit hole. Couldn't lose his focus and get sucked into the depression that sat on the edge of his psyche every damn day.

"Are you okay?"

Tommy blinked himself back to the present. "Fine. Just tired."

Sadie twisted her lips to the side. "Right, you worked the overnight shift."

He rubbed the mounting tension in his shoulders. Exhaustion dragged him down like gravity. A quick glance at the digital clock on the cable box told him he'd worked fifteen hours straight. He hadn't realized how tired he really was until he acknowledged how long he'd been working. "Yeah. I need to grab a nap soon."

Turning her back, she crouched and whipped open the cabinet under the sink. "You should go. No need to babysit me while going through this guy's place. Chances are low there's anything here anyway. You can catch up on your sleep while I finish, then we can meet up to make a game plan."

With her back to him, he didn't resist the urge to roll his eyes. "Can't wait to get rid of me?"

Standing, she faced him. "You need a break. What's the point of putting it off? The sooner you get some sleep, the sooner you'll be back to being a pain in my ass." She pressed together her lips, a small smile lifting the corners of her mouth.

"You don't have a car. It makes more sense for us to go through the trailer together then I can take you to the station before I head home."

"I'll call for someone to bring me a cruiser."

Tommy pinched the bridge of his nose. His aching muscles screamed at him to succumb to her logic and leave. Besides, even if he tried his hardest, chances of him missing something important while so damn tired were high. Sadie was capable of searching for evidence and bringing it in. Then he could help wade through whatever was found.

But even as he considered taking her offer, a part of him didn't want to give her the satisfaction. Call it childish or pigheaded, he hated leaving her to work the case alone—even if only for a couple hours.

Crossing the living room to a closed door, he cast her a wry grin. "Why don't I just crash here for a few? Then you don't have to worry about getting a car, and I can be close to help if you find something important." He fought to keep amusement from leaking into his voice. No way he'd actually sleep here, but getting a rise out of her was too damn easy.

Sadie crossed her arms over her chest. "You can't be serious."

Tommy chuckled. "We've been getting along so well. I wouldn't want you to miss me."

She moved her mouth as if her tongue coasted over her teeth. "It's incredible how you can still act like you haven't a care in the world when we're sifting through a dead man's things. A murdered man's things. It's up to us to find the killer, or can't you be bothered enough to take this seriously? I'd think you'd have more respect than that. Especially the way you lost your own mother."

Red colored his vision. "You don't know a damn thing about me or why I act the way I do. Not everyone chooses to let the tragedies of their past dictate their present. Their future. Believe me, I take this job and every case I work seriously. I just refuse to let it harden me to someone no one can stand to be around."

Pain shimmered in her eyes for a beat then quickly vanished. Tense silence filled the air.

Tommy threw up his hands. "Whatever. You want to get your own ride back into town, be my guest. I'll call you later."

Frustration boiled in his gut as he stormed out of the trailer and stomped to his car. He settled into the driver's seat and gripped his hands around the steering wheel. Dammit. He couldn't let her get to him like that. Not when they had a case to solve together. He was stuck with her for the duration, whether he liked it or not. He better find a way to deal with her.

SADIE STOOD in the now-silent trailer and stared after Tommy. She fought to keep the shaking in her hands from taking over the rest of her body. Snapping into autopilot, she lunged for the door and turned the lock. If the tremors took over, if she couldn't keep them away, she didn't want Tommy waltzing back to witness it.

She gritted her teeth, his words playing on repeat in her mind. Is that what people thought of her in this town? That she was too hard, too cold? Is that why she had a hard time getting close to anyone in Water's Edge, choosing to spend all her free time working at the shelter in Pine Valley?

She yanked off her gloves and shoved a hand through her hair, forgetting it was pulled into a ponytail, and her fingers stuck in the rubber band at the crown of her head. She yanked the band free, and her hair fell over her shoulders. She sucked in a deep breath and dropped down on the bench sandwiched between the wall and the four-person table.

What people thought of her didn't matter. Never had. She was used to living in places with few friends. She'd been doing it her whole life, and that didn't mean anything was wrong with her. She was a survivor. And she didn't need golden boy Tommy Wells' approval of who she was or how she lived.

She rubbed the tips of her middle fingers over her closed eyelids. An image of Tommy's angry scowl invaded her mind. She shook it away and opened her eyes. The man had more sides than she'd given him credit for. But what had he meant by tragedies? Losing his mother had to be difficult—she'd be lost without her own mom—but was there something else that darkened his past?

It didn't matter. She had no desire to learn about his secrets or get to know him better. His resources in helping find Shawn's killer were the only things she cared about. Something she needed to keep at the forefront of her mind from here on out.

Grabbing her phone from her back pocket, she dialed the number for the station and pushed to her feet.

"Millerton County Sheriff's Department." The voice on the other end rang out loud and clear.

"This is Deputy Sadie Pennel. I need someone to bring me my cruiser or swing by and pick me up when available."

"What's the address?"

Shit. Tommy had known where Shawn lived. She didn't have a clue what the address was, or even the street name out in the middle of nowhere. "Umm, give me a second."

A pile of loose papers took up the tabletop. Sadie rummaged through them, searching for an addressed envelope or utility bill. A bank statement caught her eye, and she shoved it to the side until she found what she needed and read the address to the deputy on the phone.

"I'll get a couple deputies to get your cruiser to you. Shouldn't take long."

She thanked him then disconnected, returning her focus to the bank statement. The numbers listed in the account summaries dropped her jaw.

Shawn was loaded.

She tossed the papers down on the table. Her wheels spun as she glanced around. Shawn had more money than she'd know in a lifetime and lived in squalor. Something didn't add up.

Sadie put her gloves back on and dug through the rest of the mostly-barren cabinets then searched every inch of the living room. She held her breath as she went through the bathroom—careful not to touch more than she had to in the rancid room. Nothing else piqued her interest like the bank statement, but she still had the bedroom.

She pushed open the flimsy door and the odor of unwashed clothes and stale food slid against her skin. She wrinkled her nose but pushed forward. Like the rest of the trailer, empty beer cans scattered along the floor. But in here, they mixed with discarded clothes and rumpled bed sheets. The queen-size bed dominated the room, the mattress was uncovered and a yellowed blanket huddled in the corner. A laptop sat on top of the bed. She'd make sure to take that into the station. Getting a closer look at Shawn's financial records was top of her priority list at the moment.

Rounding the bed, she kicked aside debris, making sure nothing of importance was hidden under the clutter. The bed sat directly on the floor. She gripped the side of the mattress and shoved it on its side, leaning it against the wall. Nothing. She lowered the mattress back down then slid open the closet door. A dresser was jammed into the space, clothes spilling out of drawers. One by one she opened them, searching for anything worth giving a second glance.

Nothing to note of inside, but a picture lay wrinkled and marred on top of the dresser. Three high school-aged guys leaning against a nice car in front of the school. She studied the youthful, smiling faces. The one in the middle was undoubtedly a young Shawn, but she wasn't sure who flanked him. Maybe Tommy would know. Hell, maybe it wouldn't even matter. If Shawn's entire life had gone downhill after he graduated high school, chances were slim he was still close to whoever was in this picture.

She flipped the photo over, interested if names or dates were scribbled on the back. Black ink wrote out a single sentence: Before I destroyed everything.

Intuition tingled the back of her neck. Maybe she hadn't

been too far off with her assumption Shawn had a secret that sent him on a downward spiral.

A distant sound reached Sadie's ears, like the rattling of a door handle. She walked to the lone window in the bedroom and peeked outside but didn't have a clear view of the driveway. The wind probably shook the trailer, causing the home to shift. A brewing sense of alarm told her to check into it.

Pulling her weapon from her side, she crept back into the living room. The door handle moved from side to side. No way the wind would make that sharp of a motion. Someone was trying to get in.

A loud thumping vibrated the trailer and rocked it back and forth. The door bent, as if someone threw themselves against the thin barrier.

Sadie's heart sputtered. Adrenaline shot through her veins. She might not know who was attempting to break into Shawn's home, but whoever it was had no idea what waited for them once they got in.

Setting her feet, she aimed her gun at the door and waited.

5

The continuous pounding against the door shook the trailer, as well as every nerve in Sadie's body. She tightened her grip on her weapon. Flashbacks of the accident in Iraq invaded her psyche and threatened to break her concentration.

But she couldn't let it.

A loud crack sounded, and the door swung open. A woman fell forward, the momentum carrying her inside.

"Police. Stop right there." Sadie commanded. Her heart hammered. Adrenaline spiked in her veins, taking away any of the tremors from moments before. "Get to your feet. Put your hands where I can see them."

"Police?" Confusion lifted the inflection of her word into a question. She clamored to her feet and lifted her palms in the air. "Is it really necessary to keep that thing pointed at me, Deputy?"

"Judge Downs?" She dropped her weapon so the barrel was pointed at the floor. "Why are you breaking into Shawn's home?"

"Please, call me Melissa." She dropped one hand and

shoved the other through blond hair that was cut in a bob at her shoulders. "I just needed to be close to Shawn, but I don't have a key. After seeing him on that metal table." She squeezed her eyes closed, her skin taking on a sickly shade of white.

Sadie rushed to her side and braced her elbow in her hand, securing her other arm along the small of Melissa's back. "Sit down. You don't look well."

Melissa plopped onto the sofa and leaned her head against the back of the couch, her face pointed toward the ceiling. "I can't believe this is happening. We wasted so much time. Spent so many years hating each other. Fighting each other. Refusing to bend or fix our shit, or hell, just let go and say goodbye. And for what?"

"Sometimes it's hard to see what the right thing is when you're stuck in the middle of a mess. I'm sure you both tried your best." She wanted to say more but hadn't gotten a chance to dive into the details of Shawn and Melissa's messy marriage. "I'm so sorry for your loss. Is there anyone you'd like me to call?"

"No. I just wanted a minute to sit here." Leaning forward, she scanned the area around her. "But this is depressing. This was the life he chose. Soaked in alcohol and covered in trash. Why would anyone want to live like this?"

The same question had kept the wheels in her head spinning since the moment she'd stepped foot in the trailer. Not knowing what else to do, she perched on the edge of the cushion. This was her chance to prove she was good at her job. That she wasn't too hard and cold to deal with a loved one of the deceased—a witness in an important investigation. Tommy might not be here, but she couldn't pass on a perfect opportunity to gain some insight. "I'm sorry to hear you and Shawn hadn't gotten along. Had you two been in an argument?"

A humorless laugh puffed from her closed mouth. "Sometimes I forget not everyone was born and raised in Water's

Edge. It's refreshing when you meet someone who doesn't already know your business. Shawn and I fell in love fast and hard, and we were so young. His mom had just died, and I'd dealt with my own loss. We bonded. We helped each other heal. But once he turned to the bottle, there was no way to reach him."

"People in pain aren't the easiest to help," Sadie said, weighing her words carefully. "I'm sure he knew how much you cared."

"I should have tried harder to mend fences, to get him help. But he wouldn't listen. Completely shut me out. Hell, he wouldn't even sign the divorce papers, as if keeping me married to him was part of my punishment. Now I'll never have a chance to make things right." She cleared her throat and wiped tears from the corners of her eyes. "You don't need to hear all this."

"Do you know if anyone wanted to hurt Shawn? Held a grudge against him?" Sadie pressed on, needing more answers.

Melissa shook her head. "I know nothing about the man he'd become these last few years. Only that he worked at the bar and was always drunk."

"What about when you two were first married? Did he get into any trouble with drugs or other dangerous activities?" Shawn and Melissa might have had a rough relationship for a while, but there had to be years where things weren't as strained. If something happened to send him over the edge, the judge might have some insight.

Melissa rubbed a palm over her jaw. "I can't think of anything that could have been a warning sign about where his life would go."

If Shawn had secrets, he obviously hadn't shared them with his estranged wife.

A soft knock tapped against the still-open door. Deputy Grant stood in the doorway. "Brought your cruiser. I'll ride back to the station with Philipps." He dipped his chin in greeting toward Melissa. "Sorry about Shawn, ma'am."

"Appreciate that."

Deputy Grant gave a stiff nod then trudged toward the waiting car in the driveway.

Turning, she offered Melissa a sad smile. "I need to get back to the station. Are you sure there's no one I can call for you to be with during this difficult time? Maybe meet you at your house?"

"I want to stay. Be close to him. Even if the place is a mess. I mean, someone needs to clean up sooner or later. No need putting it off."

She could understand wanting to feel close to someone lost too soon. When Amelia's father had died, she'd slept in his favorite sweatshirt every single night—refusing to wash it for fear it would erase the scent of his favorite cologne. She might not wear it anymore, but the shirt still sat in the back of her closet.

"I'm sorry, but I can't let you stay. There's more we need to do. Collecting evidence, dusting for fingerprints. I can't have you accidently destroying something we could use."

She nodded, the corners of her wide mouth dipping down as unshed tears hovered over her dark lashes. "I understand."

"I need to grab a few things to take into the station. Then it's best if we both leave." Sadie hustled through the space and gathered the limited items she wanted to bring in for evidence.

Most of it wouldn't amount to anything, but maybe she'd get lucky. She offered the judge a wave and hurried through the now-quickly falling snow to her car as she followed her outside. She set the bagged and labeled evidence in the back seat then climbed behind the wheel.

A heaviness settled on her shoulders as she watched Melissa Downs climb into her car and pull out onto the street. Sighing, she drove away with the image of Melissa's tortured eyes burned into her brain—an image she'd tuck away with the rest of the cruel twists of fate she'd witnessed.

TOMMY KEPT his head down and made a beeline for Sadie's desk. He'd woken to a text letting him know she was back at the station. Normally, he'd stop and chat with whoever crossed his path, but not today. Shame had kept him awake longer than he cared to admit. Snapping out of anger wasn't something he often did, even when provoked. He needed to make things right with his temporary partner.

Even if she'd deserved to take the brunt of his irritation earlier.

Sadie sat at her desk, her singular focus on her computer screen. He noted the long strands of chestnut hair flowing down her back in a low ponytail. Shallow wrinkles rippled along her freckled forehead. "Reading something interesting?"

She shot up her gaze to meet his. "Financials. Shawn's got quite a bit of money in the bank."

Tommy wheeled a chair over from the unoccupied desk beside Sadie and took a seat, slipping out of his coat and draping it behind him. "Find something at the trailer that led you to his bank account?"

"He had a bank statement sitting on the table. I called for a subpoena as soon as I left his trailer, and some strings were pulled to get it quick. Did you know the guy was loaded?" Returning her focus to the screen, she clicked the mouse to take the page back to the home screen. "Multiple accounts, and all have considerable cash. But the trust he inherited from his mother has the most. Looks like an allowance was given to him monthly until he turned twenty-five. Then it all transferred over."

Tommy studied the screen, and his jaw dropped. "He was

worth millions." He worked the math and timeline over in his head. "He's a few years older than Katherine, so he'd have gotten his hands on all that money about four years ago."

"And still lived in squalor."

"Alcoholics tend not to care much about anything except getting their hands on more booze."

Sadie ran her finger down the rows on the screen. "I don't see a steady income in here. Only the monthly deposits from the trust."

He shrugged. "Probably got paid under the table at the bar. I always wondered why Curtis kept Shawn around. Figured it was because they'd been friends since high school. Maybe it was because Shawn didn't ask for much since he didn't need it."

"Most people always want more," Sadie said. "But Shawn doesn't fit that mold. We should talk to Curtis. He might have some insight, especially since they were friends from way back."

"Want to go now? I could use a good meal before diving into whatever you found at the trailer. Curtis should be at the bar by now. We could ask him some questions while we get some grub." Nerves tightened his stomach muscles. Apologizing for being a jackass wasn't fun for him. He needed to just jump in and do it.

Raising her arms above her head, Sadie stretched and rotated her neck in a wide circle. "Sounds good. My eyes need a break. I've been looking over these accounts for a while. Besides the staggering amounts, there's not much else of interest. Lots of withdrawals, some that could be worth tracing, but I'll look at those later."

Tommy stood and put the chair back where it belonged. "Do you like looking at numbers?" He'd rather shove his head through a wall than chase a money trail by studying a computer screen. But some people lived for that shit. If Sadie was one of them, he'd let her have her fun. If not, he knew just who to ask for help.

She winced as she hopped to her feet. "Nothing worse than being stuck behind a desk, but my skills are good enough to get the job done."

He scratched the light stubble he hadn't bothered to shave. "My dad said we needed resources on this case. Mind if I pass this off to someone else so we can be in the field?"

Gratitude sparked in her eyes, and a smile twitched on her lips. "Perfect."

Tommy nodded and turned away before the stupid stirring in his gut got out of control. He was used to the shitty scowl and pissed off eyes. That combination didn't heat his blood the way this one did, and he didn't like it one bit.

Leading the way, he wove through the crowded desks and stopped at the back of the room next to Deputy Taylor Lawson. Her desk was tucked away beside the coffee station and the strong scent of burnt coffee stung his nostrils.

She didn't bother to look up from her computer, her fingers continuing to fly across the keyboard. "What do you need, Wells?"

"Got a minute to help with a murder investigation?"

She whipped up her head and excitement took over the glazed quality of her large, brown eyes. "Seriously? Whatever you want me to do has to be way more entertaining than what I've been stuck doing today. Hell, what I've done since starting here."

Tommy grinned. Taylor was his sister's best friend, and before she started working for the Miller County Sheriff's Department, she'd worked as a cybercrimes officer in Cleveland. In between that gig and this one, her list of accomplishments in the cyber world were extensive if not questionable. Working within the limits of the law put a damper on her overzealous spirit, but Taylor's need to move back to Water's

Edge to take care of her mom put her on the straight and narrow. At least for the time being.

"Did you hear about Shawn Downs?"

Taylor frowned. "Yeah. Too damn bad. I always liked him in school. He was never the same after he dropped out of college."

"Were you two friends?" Sadie asked.

Taylor shook her head. "Not really. He was older. Popular. Didn't care to show attention to an underclassman. And when I bounced into town after graduation, I stayed clear. I have enough alcoholics in my life I can't avoid. I didn't need to make conversation with another one."

Resting a hand on Taylor's shoulder, he squeezed gently before dropping his arm back to his side. Taylor's mom had been an alcoholic for as long as he could remember.

Sadie shuffled behind him. "Sorry to hear that."

Taylor tucked in her lips and shrugged. "Life throws us some curveballs. Anyway, you guys need help with Shawn's case?"

"Yeah," Tommy confirmed. "If we send you his bank information, can you dig around a little? Nothing much stands out, besides the amount of dough he has in his accounts, but there could be more than meets the eye. You'll figure out if something suspicious was happening with his withdrawals and deposits quicker than either of us, and we're itching to get in the field."

Taylor scooted forward on her chair. "Absolutely. Send everything over, and I'll get on it right away."

Sadie led the way back to her desk. She put in her passcode and brought up the account information. "Go ahead and send it over to Taylor. I don't know her email address."

Tommy leaned forward and typed in the information.

Sadie stood guard close by, as if uncomfortable giving him access to her computer. The top of her thigh pressed against him, and the smell of watermelon sanitizer wafted up his nostrils. He steeled his resolve, focusing only on the task at hand, then straightened and took a step away.

Scooping her jacket from the back of her chair, Sadie threaded her arms through the puffy sleeves. "Ready?"

"One thing first."

She hooked up an eyebrow.

He coughed, hoping to clear the tension from his throat while he searched for the right words. "Sorry for snapping at you earlier. I could blame being tired and cranky, but that's no excuse. I was rude and unprofessional. I won't let it happen again."

Surprise colored her peaches and cream complexion. "Thank you. But I shouldn't have said what I did. Let's agree we both crossed a line and promise to not do it again."

"Agreed." He extended a hand.

She clasped her palm to his.

He curled his fingers around her smooth skin, and a bolt of electricity shot up his arm.

She yanked away her hand and dropped her gaze to the laminate floor.

She felt it too.

He cleared his throat, grabbed his jacket, and started for the door. Whatever the hell just happened, he didn't want to waste time on it. Just like his behavior earlier, the heat from Sadie's touch was something he'd never let happen again—he wouldn't allow himself to get that close.

6

Muted rays of sunlight barely infiltrated the thick snow clouds, making the hour seem much later. But even that tiny bit of light didn't sneak inside Town Tavern as Sadie entered the bar. She blinked to adjust to the dim atmosphere. No one had been allowed to smoke in here for years, but the stale cigarette scent had penetrated the walls and still hung in the air. The clinking of pool balls sounded on the far end of the wide-open room. A scattering of square tables sat between the distant billiards and the aged wooden bar that dominated the entire wall to the right.

"Do you want to sit at a table or is the bar okay?" Tommy asked.

Sitting alone with him at one of the tables amid the rest of the early dinner crowd, no matter how small, gave an impression that made her skin itch. "The bar's fine. Then we can chat with Curtis while he's working. He might be willing to answer more questions if we don't pull him away from his job."

Tommy led the way to the backless stools tucked under the lip of the bar and took a seat.

Sadie settled in beside him and grabbed a plastic menu

wedged between bottles of ketchup and mustard. Her stomach growled. The protein bar she'd scarfed down for lunch hadn't done much for her appetite. Scanning the food items, she mentally made her choice and waited for the bar owner to take her order.

Curtis acknowledged them with a nod as he pulled on one of four taps, filling a glass to the brim with amber liquid.

"Do you want to look at the menu?" She wiggled the plastic sheet in front of Tommy.

"Nah. I come here a couple times a week. Pretty much have the thing memorized."

"I didn't realize you spent so much of your free time at the bar." She shouldn't be surprised. Water's Edge didn't have many options for entertainment. An old movie theater that had one screen and held maybe fifty people, a bowling alley where most of the high school-aged crowd gathered on the weekend, and Town Tavern.

She may not frequent many of those places around town, spending all her time outside work with Amelia or at the shelter, but Tommy would need more than a cartoon movie and bowl of popcorn to entertain him.

"It's the best place to come for local gossip," Tommy said, cutting into her thoughts.

She wrinkled her nose and tried to hide her amusement at the image of Tommy with his head bent low beside the blue-haired women in town, trading secrets.

He chuckled and bounced his shoulder off hers. "Not in a listening to grandma spreading rumors after church kind of way. A lot of people stop by over the course of the week. Talking about who got laid off, who's having issues in their marriage. It helps me keep a pulse on things around here. Find out where I can give back a little."

"Give back?"

He shrugged. "Never know who might need an extra hand. I

even tried to talk Shawn into AA, hoping to get him to a better place."

Sadie locked her gaze on the weathered wood in front of her, unable to find any words. First, he'd blown her away for apologizing after being a dick—an apology she didn't completely deserve since she'd let him push her buttons and had lashed out. Now he admitted to checking up on citizens in his free time.

She chose to volunteer at the shelter because it was a cause close to her heart and also gave her the opportunity to give back. He'd shown up with his brother and Marie from time to time, doling out donations like he had the night before or clowning around for get-togethers. Never in a million years did she expect he'd donate his time to really help others.

"Hey, Tommy, what can I do ya for?" Curtis grabbed a white dishtowel from over his shoulder and wiped down the bar. "A little early for dinner."

"Schedule's weird today. Worked the night shift, then caught a case this morning. I grabbed a few hours rest, but back at it. Nothing like one of your bacon cheeseburgers to put me in the right state of mind to get shit done."

A gravelly laugh boomed from Curtis—the kind that came from smoking a pack a day—then his mouth dropped into a frown. "Wait a minute. Are you talking about Shawn?"

Tommy cocked his head toward her. "Deputy Pennel's the one who found him. We're both working the case."

Understanding shone through the grief in his eyes. "You're here to ask me questions."

"Just the basics," Sadie said, the need to assert herself pressing down on her lungs.

Curtis drew in a large breath. "I figured someone would be by. Why don't I get your orders then I'll swing around and give you guys as much time as you need. Deputy Pennel, do you know what you want?"

She'd settled on a salad, but Tommy's order made her change her mind. "I'll have what Tommy's having. Throw in some fries and a cola."

"Same," Tommy said.

Curtis headed toward the swinging door that led to the kitchen.

Tommy propped his elbows on the countertop. "How about we figure out a game plan while we wait for Curtis? We should also figure out a time to speak with Melissa Downs again soon."

She shifted on the hard stool. The beginning of this partnership was harder than hurling flurries during a snowstorm, but they'd finally reached a truce and agreed to move forward. Admitting she talked to the judge could ruffle his feathers and put her and Tommy right back on a path filled with animosity. But she had to tell him. "Melissa Downs stopped by Shawn's trailer after you left."

"What? Why?" Confusion instead of anger lifted his voice, loosening the knots in her stomach.

"She wanted to be close to Shawn. She scared the crap out of me, actually. She didn't have a key and tried to break in. I was waiting for her in the living room with a gun in my hands."

He faced her with wide eyes. "You pulled a gun on the county judge?"

She cringed. "I don't want to talk about it."

He grinned. "Fine. What happened? Did you talk to her?"

"I asked some questions. If she knew of anyone who wanted to hurt Shawn, she didn't offer any insight. The conversation was brief. I told her the two of us would be by to talk with her more, but we might want to give her a day or so."

"I agree. Did you find anything else at Shawn's?"

She shrugged. "A few things, but not sure it'll amount to much. The money's the big thing. I also found a picture of him and a couple other guys that he wrote on the back of. It said, 'Before I ruined everything.'"

"I'd like to see that. Figure out who he was with. What about electronics?"

"He had a laptop. It's at the station and still needs to be looked over."

"How about we head back to the station when we're done here? I'd like to see what's on the computer before we make our next move. There could be something that points in the right direction."

The kitchen door swung open, and Curtis stepped through the doorway with a plate in each hand. The smell of the angus patties and French fries made it to her before the bar owner did. Her mouth watered. "Good plan. Now let's focus on Curtis. An old friend of Shawn's from high school who saw Shawn almost every day should have a lot of information." She kept her voice low so Curtis wouldn't hear.

Tommy tightened his jaw, his gaze fixed on Curtis.

Awareness crept along the back of her neck. Did Tommy think Curtis held the key to figuring out what happened to Shawn because the two were friends, or because Curtis might have known Shawn well enough to discover his secrets?

Secrets that could lead to murder.

"WOULD you rather talk here or grab a table?" Tommy asked as Curtis set a plate in front of him.

Curtis glanced around the mostly empty room. "Here's fine. Ashley won't come in to serve tables for another hour, and Tony's in the kitchen prepping for dinner. I need to be able to see what's going on. Give me a second, and I'll grab your sodas."

Sadie slid her plate closer. "What's your take on this guy?"

"Never been in trouble with the law, as far as I know. Don't know too much about him. Seems nice enough." Tommy kept his voice low and gaze locked on Curtis' profile as he filled two glasses a few feet away. "He's probably the closest friend Shawn had."

"Do you think he knows something?"

Tommy faced her and shrugged. "If there's anyone who can gives us dirt, it's Curtis. I'm just not sure if that dirt ended up on Curtis's hands or not."

God, he hoped not. But the possibility of Curtis hurting Shawn had crossed his mind. When a harmless drunk only socialized with a handful of people, the pool of suspects was pretty small. Someone wouldn't hunt him down in the middle of a meadow for a good time. Someone was pissed.

Pissed enough to end Shawn's life. And chances were that pissed off person was someone who knew a hell of a lot about Shawn.

Curtis returned with their drinks then leaned against the bar. "So, what do you want to know?"

"How long has Shawn worked for you?" Sadie asked then bit into the end of a long fry.

Curtis scratched his jaw. "Let's see. I bought the place about seven years ago. Shawn was here since the beginning."

"And did you think it was a good idea to give an alcoholic a job at a bar? Was Shawn's drinking ever a problem?" Sadie pressed.

Tommy took a bite of his burger, an eruption of gooey cheese and salty meat exploding on his tongue. He'd let her take the lead—something she obviously thought was important—and just listen while he ate. At least for the moment.

Curtis narrowed his beady eyes. "He wasn't always such a mess, okay. We were friends since we were kids. He needed help, and I could lend him a hand by giving him a job. He never caused any problems for anyone."

Sadie took a sip of her soda before asking another question. "He never had issues with anyone in here? Made anyone mad? Get on anyone's bad side?"

Curtis shot his hand through his scraggly dirty blond hair. "Not that I can recall." Dropping his gaze, he rubbed his thumb over a groove in the bar.

Tommy set down his burger and studied Curtis. *He's hiding something.* Tommy folded his hands and rested them on the worn wood in front of his plate. "Listen. You two were close, had been for years, anything you know could help us find out who killed him. If you say he didn't start shit with anyone at the bar, fine. But what about outside of work? Had he talked about getting into trouble recently? Anything off in his demeanor?"

"His demeanor's been off for years." Curtis licked his thin lips and darted his gaze around the room. He leaned forward, pressing his too-thin middle against the scarred wooden counter. "But there is one thing. He talked about Clara a lot lately."

"Clara Parson?"

"Who's that?" Sadie asked.

Curtis spared her a glance. "We went to school with her. She's married to one of our best friends from way back. She and Shawn dated when they were teenagers."

"Did Shawn and Mitch still talk?" Tommy didn't know much about Mitch Parson except he was a teacher at the local high school and was known to have one hell of a temper. More than one call had been made to the station by neighbors because of his yelling at his wife.

"They hadn't talked for years. Not that I know of, anyway. Mitch distanced himself when Shawn started his downhill spiral. Didn't want it to cast any negative attention on him when he was starting his career."

"Do you think Shawn and Clara were talking? Seeing each other?" If Shawn made a play on another man's wife—a man with a history of a temper—then they just found another lead. Not to mention how that could piss off the woman he was still married too, estranged or not.

Curtis shrugged. "He never said, but if I had to guess, something was going on. A man doesn't just start talking about a woman from his past for no reason."

"We'll talk to her." Sadie cast a quick glance at Tommy. "No need to alert her husband to anything his wife may or may not have done before we get her side of the story."

Tommy nodded. "Agreed."

"Is there anything else you can think of? No matter how small it seems." Sadie sliced a knife through the center of her burger, cutting it in two.

"No, but if I think of anything, I swear I'll tell you. Shawn had his issues, but deep down, he was a good guy. He didn't deserve this." The door opened and a middle-aged couple strolled in and took a seat at a booth on the opposite wall. "I've got to take their order. Your food's getting cold anyway. Eat, and I'll call if anything comes to mind."

Tommy dipped a few fries in a glob of ketchup and stuffed them in his mouth.

With her elbows propped on the bar, Sadie picked up half her burger. "What do you think? Would this Clara woman cheat on her husband with a guy like Shawn?" She bit into her sandwich and moaned. "Damn, this is good."

"Maybe. They have a history. I want to talk to my sister. She might have a better idea of the dynamics between the group from high school. Might know why Shawn and Clara broke up, or if the split was bad enough to keep the two away from each other for good."

"Seems odd she married her ex's good friend."

Tommy shrugged. "It's a small town. If people stay here, there aren't too many options. They're bound to end up with someone that a friend dated at some point."

She quirked her lips, questions shooting from her eyes.

Questions he had no intentions of answering. He might be from Water's Edge and familiar with the small pool of potential dates, but he didn't give two shits about dating. He'd lost not one, but two women he loved. He didn't have it in him to lose a third.

"Mitch is a teacher, so Clara should be free to talk to us tomorrow while he's at work. She stays home with their kids. Why don't we stop by in the morning and get the scoop on her and Shawn?" His stomach growling, he bit into his burger, ending any further conversation. He wanted to finish his meal and get the hell out of here. They gotten what they needed from Curtis—for now—and had work waiting for them back at the station.

As if reading his mind, Sadie dug into the rest of her food without another word. When she finished, she pushed away the plate and ran a hand over her flat stomach. "I won't need to eat anything else until tomorrow."

Tommy chuckled and dabbed a napkin on his mouth. He threw the dirty napkin on his empty plate. "Same. Ready to head out?"

She nodded and climbed off the stool.

He threw some bills on the counter and followed her to the door, casting a quick wave at Curtis, who was back behind the bar, before pushing open the door for Sadie. A gust of wind slammed against them. He huddled inside his jacket, wishing the station was closer than the two blocks they had to walk.

A buzz vibrated against his thigh, and he grabbed his phone from his pocket. A text message from Taylor. He swiped it open, wishing he'd donned gloves on his freezing hands, and read her message. "Well, shit."

Sadie halted in the middle of the sidewalk. "What happened?"

He sighed. "Shawn didn't have any income from the bar, but the bar was getting money from Shawn."

She furrowed her brow and thick snowflakes nestled in her hair. "What do you mean?"

He handed her the phone so she could read Taylor's message for herself. "Shawn paid Curtis a thousand dollars a month. Has been for years."

Tommy fisted his hands inside his coat pocket. Now they had two leads to follow. One possibly involving sex, the other money. Both damn good reasons to kill.

7

White lights ran across the roof and wrapped around the porch of Safe Haven Women's Shelter. A large green wreath dotted with holly and red velvet bows hung on the door. Sadie stepped out of her car and into the lightly falling snow, taking her time on the short walk inside.

The day had been long, and tension bunched the muscles in her shoulders. The fifteen-minute drive to Pine Valley was all she'd get to herself, her only time to unwind and clear her head. Once she entered the large Victorian house and wrapped her arms around Amelia, mom mode would be all consuming until she slipped into sleep later that night.

But she wouldn't have it any other way.

Once on the porch, she stomped the snow off her boots and entered the foyer. A hum of activity reached her ears from behind the swinging door that led to the kitchen. She smiled, the muted melody of a holiday song barely audible, but the giggles undeniable.

She filled her lungs on a deep breath. This shelter brought more than just a safe place to women who found themselves in bad situations. It brought peace and joy to her every time she stepped inside.

With a renewed spirit, Sadie hurried into the kitchen where the scents of lemon and garlic mingled with fresh baked cookies. An odd yet charming aroma, especially combined with the cheerful scene at the neatly set table. Mrs. Collins stood in front of the stove and plated breaded chicken while Laura strapped her daughter, Isla, into a highchair.

"Mama!" Amelia launched herself from where she sat on the bench seat and burrowed into Sadie's arms.

Sadie cuddled her close, soaking in every ounce of sweet, ornery goodness. "I see you talked Mrs. Collins into baking those cookies today."

Laura brushed a long strand of hair off her forehead with the back of her wrist. "Those cookies were a joint effort, weren't they, Amelia? I'm not letting Mrs. Collins take all the credit."

Sadie kissed Amelia's forehead. "Thanks for watching her. I caught a big case, so the next few days might be a little hectic. Are you sure you're fine with me bringing her here while I work? I can make other arrangements for her school break."

"Are you taking about Shawn Downs?" Laura asked, frowning.

Sadie nodded, not wanting to say more in front of Amelia. She always tried to keep her work life as separate as possible from her daughter. Amelia didn't need to be aware of all the bad things happening in the world around her.

At least not yet.

"Marie mentioned it before she headed home. Said Owen spoke with Tommy a little about the case." With Isla safely secured in her chair, Laura crossed to the island and pulled silverware from the drawer. "You two staying for dinner?"

Sadie hesitated. The idea of going home and preparing a meal was less appealing than watching paint dry, but these women had already done enough for her today.

"Of course they are." Mrs. Collins grabbed the platter of chicken and headed to the table. She placed it on the red and green plaid runner. "Amelia helped make the salad. She has to eat it. That was the deal."

Amelia scrunched her nose. "Can I pick out the tomatoes? They make my tongue feel funny."

Mrs. Collins twisted her lips to the side as if giving the question careful consideration. "Fine. As long as you eat all your chicken."

"Deal!" Amelia jumped back into her seat. "Sit by me, Mama."

"Are you sure there's enough food?" she asked, settling in beside her daughter. The colorful vegetables in the salad and scent of parmesan crusted chicken made her mouth water. She hoped the answer to her question was yes because no way she could leave without sampling the food now.

"There's plenty. The guest who came last night is in her room. Dr. Simon is stopping by soon to speak with her and look over some injuries. She doesn't plan to come down for dinner, but I put aside some food I'll take up later." Mrs. Collins sat at the head of the table and passed bowls and platters around, helping to fill plates for the children.

"Did Marie mention anything else regarding what Owen said about Shawn?" Sadie was unable to stop herself from asking the question as she doused her salad with dressing. Tommy's older brother was also a sheriff's deputy and closer to Shawn's age. He may have slipped details to Marie that could be beneficial.

"Not really. Or at least Marie didn't say much. Just that she was relieved he wasn't on the case and would be home tonight." Laura used a fork to mash a banana on Isla's tray before buttering a roll and placing it on the side of her plate. "I made sure to get here as backup right before she took off. Isla was thrilled to see her best friend, Amelia. Weren't ya, honey?"

Isla squealed and smashed her food into her mouth.

Amelia giggled. "She's so messy."

Sadie debated asking Laura or Mrs. Collins if they knew anything about Shawn Downs. They'd both lived in Pine Valley their entire lives so it wasn't farfetched to think news could travel down the mountain road to their town.

But this wasn't the time or the place. This was a place for her to let her guard down and leave her troubles from work behind her. A place to sit and eat and visit with people she cared about and who cared for not only her, but her child as well.

Warmth finally chased the chill of the awful day from Sadie's bones. This was her home, her family. A community she'd found who always stood beside her, helping her in whatever way they could. She'd swallow whatever questions swam in her mind about Shawn Downs and just enjoy her friends and a fabulous meal.

TOMMY INHALED a deep breath of crisp, fresh air before stepping into the putrid atmosphere of Shawn's trailer. After Sadie headed home for the evening, he decided to stop by and comb through the trailer one more time. He had nowhere else to be, and he couldn't shake the feeling they'd missed something.

As he stepped into Shawn's home, he pulled out his phone to call Katherine. Energy whirled through his limbs. No way he'd get his wheels to stop spinning. After he left the trailer, he might as well swing by Katherine's and have a quick visit to talk to her about Shawn's old buddies.

Besides, he hadn't gotten to see his nephew in a few days. He'd use any excuse to visit with Oliver. He punched in Katherine's contact information and waited for her to answer as he went through the living room.

"Hey, Tommy. What's up?" Katherine's voice came through the speaker clipped and distracted.

"You okay?" He unzipped his jacket but left it on, not trusting any surface in the space to be free of grime.

"Hmm-hmm."

He chuckled. "Bad time? Do you want me to call you later?" He swiped his gloved hand under the dirty couch palm up.

"Sorry. Just a little distracted. How are you?"

"Fine. I'm at Shawn Downs' place. I wanted to give the space a look myself. Had to take off earlier when I came with Deputy Pennel." Nothing but metal springs brushed against his hand. He straightened and tossed the cushions to the floor. Empty chip bags and a plethora of crumbs strewn everywhere. "The guy lived like a pig."

"Doesn't surprise me." A tinge of sadness coated her statement. "His life was a mess, so why wouldn't his home be as well?"

"True. Did you know him? He was closer to your age than mine or Owen's." He gave the room one last survey then moved on to the bedroom.

"I knew him a little when we were younger. I haven't spoken with him in years, though."

Tommy kicked at the mounds of blankets on the floor and poked around the bed and closet. "What about his friends from high school?"

"Umm, a little. I didn't spend much time with them. But we were acquainted. You know how it is around here. Everyone knows everyone's business."

Not finding anything, he hurried to the kitchen. "I'd like to talk to you about it, if you're free this evening. I can come over when I'm done here."

Katherine chuckled. "Do you really think you need to come

over to have this conversation, or do you just want to see Oliver?"

He peeked through the open cabinets then stepped into the bathroom. The scent of something rotten wrinkled his nose the moment he crossed the threshold, and he covered his nostrils with his elbow. "You caught me."

He backed out of the bathroom and glanced at the digital clock on the cable box. "He won't be in bed yet, will he?" It was just past 8:00 pm on a school night. Katherine and her husband Theo had a fairly strict routine for their five-year-old son, and he didn't want to intrude.

"I'll make sure he's still awake when you get here. At least for a little bit. So, have you found anything? I can hear you rummaging around."

He fought the urge to run his hand over his face, not wanting the dirt and germs from his glove on him. "Nothing. Deputy Pennel swept through earlier, so I didn't expect to find something important in an obvious place. But I thought maybe she missed something."

"You're at his trailer, right?" Katherine asked.

"Yeah. I'm going to take off. This is pointless." He swept the area with his gaze one last time.

"What about outside? Does he have a shed or anything? Did you check under the home? Trailers sit up a little bit. He could have hidden something underneath."

"I'll check outside then head to your place. Should be there in about fifteen minutes or so."

Zipping his jacket, he resealed the scene and filled his lungs with clean air once he stepped outside. He studied the bottom of the trailer. Cinder blocks kept the structure off the ground. He trudged through the snow and circled to the back of the trailer, noting the empty bottles thrown into the woods. He grabbed the penlight he kept in the inside pocket of his coat and crouched. The narrow light cut through the darkness. Nothing stood out but a tangle of dried weeds and more trash.

Straightening, he swept the light over the rusted siding. A small slit in one of the seams caught his attention. He ran his fingers between the loosening siding. He applied more pressure, slipping his hand in the slot. Something brushed against the pad of his index finger, and he dug deeper. Pinching whatever was lodged inside, he pulled it out. Sheets of paper flapped in the whipping breeze and a lone key fell into his hand.

His pulse raced. Shawn wouldn't have gone through the trouble of hiding whatever the hell this was in the siding of his house for nothing. Jumping in the car, he cranked the heat and carefully peeled apart the paper. Some sheets were lined from a notebook while others were plain white, like the kind used in a printer. Ripped edges and scraps of paper torn from menus and newspapers. Sketches and drawings filled the pages. Shawn had talent, even if his artistic endeavors tilted more toward creepy and sinister.

Sketches of devils with pitch forks, car crashes, and execution-styled shootings were graphic and disturbing. Tommy shuffled through, making note of words and names, but there was no way he could get through all the pages and pictures sitting in his car. Flicking his thumb over the edge of the pile, he flipped the paper quickly. There were countless doodles and drawings to study, analyze, and try to decipher.

He switched his focus to the key. Nothing in the trailer could be locked beside the front door, and this was too small to fit into the handle. His financial records didn't indicate a deposit box at the bank, but he'd ask Taylor if she'd found one that flew under the radar. Other than that, he had no idea what the key was for, but he'd damn sure find out.

The time lit the dashboard. He needed to get to Katherine's if he wanted a chance to see Oliver. Sealing the papers and key in an evidence bag, he tossed it on the seat beside him then yanked the soiled gloves from his hands. This was big. They now had an inside image of Shawn's mind and possibly what he was involved in.

And if it weren't for Katherine, he wouldn't have even checked the outside of the trailer. He'd have to drive through The Creamery and grab Katherine's favorite treat as a thank you. It wouldn't matter that the temperatures were below freezing. She'd never say no to ice cream. He could grab something for Oliver and Theo, too. He smiled. A surge of sugar would be perfect before putting the kid to bed.

The full moon was bright in the now-clear sky, reflecting the white peaks of the mountains that loomed ahead. The snow had stopped while he'd been inside the trailer, but the roads hadn't been cleared. Gripping the wheel, he kept his speed slow. The last thing he needed was to slide through the slush and end up in the deep ditch on the side of the road.

Pushing the hidden drawings and key to the back of his mind, he refocused his thoughts on the dynamics of Shawn's high school group of friends. He had a host of questions for Katherine and didn't want to forget anything. Most importantly, he wanted the dirt on the relationship between Shawn and Clara and if Katherine thought they'd rekindled a romance—even though Clara and Shawn were both married, and Shawn was a drunk.

A train whistle trilled in the distance. Stars twinkled overhead, shining down on the town as he approached the south edge of the city limits. He'd grab the treats and be at Katherine's in less than ten minutes. Hopefully, he'd leave with a better picture of the boy Shawn used to be.

A flash of red lights blinked into the dark night, alerting Tommy to the railroad tracks up ahead. He slowed and stopped in front of the lowered gate, separating him from the tracks.

Sighing, Tommy ran a hand over his face, resting it along his jawline as he propped his elbow on the door and pressed his foot on the brake. His nerves jingled, matching the rhythm of the strobing lights by the sign. Working an overnight shift then following up with a day shift, regardless of the small nap he snuck in, had messed with his entire system. If he could get a solid night's sleep, hopefully it would set his internal clock straight.

A glare bounced off his rearview mirror. Tommy turned to glance out the back window. Headlights came toward him. Facing forward again, he fiddled with the radio until a classic rock song blared through the speakers.

The shrill whistle sounded again, closer as it barreled down the tracks.

He glanced out the driver's side window. A line of trees stood in front of the tracks for as far as he could see, glimpses of the fast-moving train appearing in flashes between the barren branches. He bounced his knee up and down, impatience swarming inside his body.

The headlights came closer.

Tommy checked the back window again, and his heartrate sped up faster than the approaching train. The vehicle behind him closed in, filling the gap between them quickly. He squinted, trying to make out the car, but the headlights were too bright to see beyond the blinding light.

The whistle blew louder, the bells chimed in warning. Tommy pressed the palm of his hand against his horn. Maybe whoever was behind the wheel wasn't paying attention or had fallen asleep.

The driver wasn't slowing. If the asshole didn't stop soon, he'd get rear ended.

Lights poured through Tommy's car. The train getting closer, the large white barrier preventing him from pulling forward and away from the lunatic behind him. Sweat beaded his temple.

A truck slammed into Tommy's bumper. Metal crashed

against metal, the screeching sound piercing his eardrums. The airbag erupted, pushing into his chest. Sharp pain exploded in his ribs. His head lurched forward. Whiplash pulled his neck muscles. His head screamed in pain. His foot slipped off the brake pedal, and an engine revved behind him. The truck continued to push against the back of his car.

Tommy's car shot forward. He blinked, trying to gain his bearings, but the pain whacking against his skull made it hard to concentrate. The white barrier came closer, his car pushing against the only protection between him and the train speeding down the tracks. The hood of his cruiser drifted under the barrier, the white beam smacking into his windshield. The wooden bar creaked, straining against his still-moving car, until it cracked. The truck propelled him onto the track then stopped, blocking his means of escape.

He stretched his neck to the side and caught a glimpse of the big black train coming straight at him.

8

The whistle came closer, louder. Tommy had to do something. Fast. The deployed airbag made moving his arms difficult. He needed to deflate the bag before it pushed all the air from his lungs. His arm ached, but he wiggled it to the center console and secured his pocketknife in his hand. He slashed the blade through the material.

The bag deflated, and he pushed it aside. He spared a quick look out his window. The large black train was seconds away.

Tommy slammed his foot on the gas and shot forward, crashing through the wooden gate on the opposite side of the track. The ground vibrated and the thumping of the train trembled behind him. Tremors overtook his body, but he couldn't just sit there. He had to know who'd just tried to kill him.

Pushing open the door, he stumbled out of the car. He cradled his injured ribs with a shaking arm as he faced the quick-flying cars of the train. Through flashes of the scene ahead, only the taillights of the retreating truck gave any hints of who had come after him. Not even the color of the large vehicle was clear in the dark night.

A shaky breath left his body. He hunched over and rested

his forearms on his knees. The wind from the speeding train mixed with the frigid air, but he didn't mind. He needed it to cool the flames of turmoil licking inside his stomach.

Straightening, he grabbed his phone and called dispatch to report the incident. The crime scene unit might be able to identify the tread marks on the snow-covered street. He'd walk over and mark off a good section of the road after the train passed to make sure no other vehicles contaminated the tracks with their own.

After relaying the information to dispatch, he called Katherine. He needed to let her know he wouldn't be stopping by. Plus, just hearing her voice might help calm his tangled nerves. She was always the one he turned to when he was upset. After their mom died, Katherine had become the one he leaned on, while his dad had buried himself in work, his brother tried to please everyone, and his grandparents lost themselves in grief.

"You almost here?" Katherine picked up after the first ring.

"No." His voice came out thick, like cotton balls were wedged in his throat. "Someone pushed my cruiser onto the train tracks just south of town."

"What?" The word exploded on the line. "On purpose?"

"No doubt." He crouched in front of the damaged back end of his car. He'd need a tow truck to take his cruiser to an autobody shop. "Bastard turned around and high-tailed it out of here. Police are on the way."

"I'm coming. Don't even try to argue."

He chuckled, and his ribs ached. "I know better than to take on any argument with you. But it's really not necessary. By the time you get here, backup will have arrived and I can get a ride from whatever deputy shows up on scene."

"Why do you need a ride?"

He let his gaze roam over the crunched metal of his vehicle again. "My car might be totaled. For sure can't drive it now."

She sucked in a breath. "Are you okay? Are the paramedics coming, too?"

"I'm a little banged up. Nothing major." Not like he'd tell if that wasn't true. No reason to worry her if he was all right. "I'm sure an ambulance is on the way. I'll get checked out."

"I need to fill in Theo, then I'll be there. Hold tight."

"Katherine, really, stay home. It's late and cold. I'll come see you tomorrow. I promise."

"Fine." The reluctance in her voice told him how hard it was to stay put. "But call if you need anything. I love you. Stay safe."

"I love you, too." He put his phone back in his pocket and watched the last of the train fly by. Making sure the coast was clear, he limped to the center of the tracks. Bits and pieces of smashed metal from his car littered the ground. He kicked the bits of wreckage aside, shining a light on the debris, but nothing appeared to be useful in identifying the make or model of the truck—or who'd been behind the wheel.

Sirens pierced the night. Tommy walked toward the approaching emergency vehicles coming from the center of town. A cruiser and an ambulance stopped on the side of the road and parked in front of his ruined car. Tommy spied a wide-brimmed hat on the head of the large man behind the wheel of the cruiser and groaned.

Sheriff Mike Wells, his father, stepped out of his car with a hard scowl on his doughy face. His eyes met Tommy's as he hurried over.

Tommy straightened and tried not to wince. He hadn't lied when telling Katherine he was fine, but that didn't mean his whole body didn't hurt like a bitch. But he couldn't let his dad notice, or he'd make a bigger deal than necessary.

Mike stopped in front of him, sparing a quick glance at the car. "What in the world happened?"

"I'm surprised whoever called you didn't fill you in."

Mike pressed his thin lips together. "I got the gist, but I'd like to hear what happened from you."

Suppressing a sigh, Tommy divulged every detail. The emergency medic jogged toward him, but Tommy lifted a hand to indicate the younger man had to wait. He needed his dad to take him seriously—to see him as a competent lawman—and he couldn't exude that image with a medic buzzing around checking his injuries.

By the time Tommy finished, his limbs shook and the pain in his head had intensified tenfold. He leaned against the hood of his car, hoping it would keep him upright.

"Shit." Mike took off his hat and ran a hand over his balding head. "You're right. Definitely not an accident. Who would want to hurt you? Piss anyone off lately?"

"I really need to take a look at you now," Eric said and unlooped a stethoscope from around his neck. "I can do the initial evaluation while you talk, but I need you in the back of the ambulance for a more thorough check when you're done. You're pretty banged up."

"Fine." Tommy stood still and let Eric do his job while he continued his conversation with his dad—but dammit if it wasn't distracting to have the other man flapping around him. "Not that I know of. The last big case I helped with, the bad guy ended up dead. But Owen was the lead on that case, not me."

"What about small crimes. Something a guy—or girl—could hold a grudge over?"

He thought back over his recent caseload but nothing but parking tickets and busting up a high-school party came to mind. "Nothing."

Mike glanced past Tommy. "Where were you coming from?"

A car door slammed. Another cruiser had driven up while he talked to his dad and parked behind the slashing red lights of the ambulance. "I was at Shawn Downs' place. I was heading back to town and going to stop at Katherine's before I went home."

Eric took a step back. "Looks like superficial wounds. But I'll meet you in my truck when you're done." He gave a nod and retreated to the ambulance.

A familiar silhouette trudged forward at a clipped pace. Sadie closed the distance between them, her round face pinched tight in either concern or anger.

"Did you notice anyone lingering around Shawn's place? Anyone follow you after you left?" Mike asked.

Sadie stopped beside Mike and crossed her arms over her chest. "Are you okay?"

Tommy lifted a shoulder. "Not too bad."

"Good, then I don't have to feel bad for asking you what you were doing at Shawn's alone."

He sighed and bounced his gaze between his dad and his temporary partner. With his head pounding and ribs aching, the last thing he wanted to do was have this conversation with either one of them.

SADIE KEPT Amelia's hand tucked in hers as they followed Tommy up the ancient stairs to his apartment. He rented a place above the local pizza shop in downtown Water's Edge, and the smell of garlic and oregano hung heavy in the air. He moved slow, obviously in more pain than he'd let on to her or the emergency worker.

"I wish we lived in a pizza place," Amelia whispered, awe clear in her little voice.

She smiled down at her daughter and squeezed her hand. "Dream big, little one."

Tommy grinned over his shoulder, and she barely made out

the bruise on his cheekbone in the dimly lit stairwell. "Trust me, it's not all it's cracked up to be. Everything I own smells like cheese."

Amelia giggled.

"Thanks for walking me home, ladies, but I can take it from here."

"I want to smell your cheesy apartment." Amelia let go of Sadie's hand and grabbed hold of Tommy's "Please."

Normally she'd scold Amelia for nagging, but she was determined to get Tommy situated and see for herself he was fine before leaving. When her police scanner had announced his accident on her way home from the shelter she hadn't thought, just moved on instinct.

And instinct had driven her and Amelia straight to Tommy.

He insisted he wasn't hurt too bad, but his slight limp and the circles under his eyes told a different story. Before she could take Amelia home, she had to make sure he had everything he needed to tend to his cuts and bruises.

Tommy grinned down at Amelia, but Sadie could see how hard it was for him not to wince. "How can I say no to such a polite girl?" He unlocked and pushed open his door, letting Amelia in front of him.

Amelia ran inside. "You're silly. It doesn't smell like cheese, but it is messy. Mama never lets my room get this messy."

"Glad to know." Tommy chuckled and shrugged out of his jacket.

Sadie moved passed him into the small living room that flowed right into the kitchen. Her gaze landed on the empty takeout containers on the granite countertop, the smattering of papers littered across the two-person table stuffed in a corner, and the cozy blanket draped over the back of the leather couch.

Amelia was right. No way she'd let so much clutter linger in any room of their tidy home.

"Do you want to help Tommy clean up? You know how to throw away trash. I'm sure it'd be a huge help." Sadie was of a firm belief that a clean home created a clean mind. She'd spent so many years with nothing that she took great care of the things she now owned, and she wanted to teach that lesson to her daughter as well.

"Can I?" Amelia asked, bouncing on her toes with excitement as if she'd told the girl she could throw glitter in the air.

"You don't have to do that," Tommy said. "I'll get to it tomorrow."

Sadie hooked a brow. "Doubtful. It's a nice apartment though. Not what I expected."

An earthy green covered the walls, complimenting the masculine tones in the space. Little bits of clutter sat on most surfaces, but the place smelled of lemon disinfectant. Messy, but clean. She bet if she stepped into his bedroom, she'd find the bed unmade, but at least the sheets would be recently washed.

Warmth flooded her cheeks. She couldn't let her mind wander to what she'd find in Tommy's bedroom. He was in the *don't touch, don't look, don't even think about it* part of her brain.

Brushing past her, Tommy slid off his jacket and tossed it on top of the colorful blanket. He turned and leaned against the couch, fixing his tired eyes on her. "You've thought about my place, huh?"

Shaking her head, she smirked. "Not even a little."

Tommy grinned then glanced over at Amelia in the kitchen, busy as a bee. "I'm sorry. But I had to go to Shawn's myself."

She crossed her arms. "You didn't think I could be trusted to do a good job?"

"That's not it." He rubbed his forehead, just above his eyes.

A pinch of guilt burrowed into her stomach. He'd been through a lot tonight. She didn't even want to examine the fear that had grabbed her by the throat when she'd heard the call come through on the scanner.

She rounded the edge of the sofa and opted to sit in the recliner, angling to keep an eye on Amelia. "I want to know my partner trusts me. That he knows I'm damn good at my job."

Tommy sank down on the couch. "I do know that. But my mind was spinning, and I had to do something. I found myself back there, going through his stuff. I found this." Grabbing his jacket, he pulled an evidence bag from the pocket.

She leaned forward and took the bag. Staring through the clear plastic, she tried to give meaning behind the scraps of paper inside. "What is this?"

"Drawings. Sketches. Weird ass comments. I didn't go through all of them, but it's enough to realize something had Shawn twisted inside. We need to look at every scratch mark on those pages. Shawn might be the only one who can point us in the right direction—even if he isn't here. Then there's the random key. No clue what that will unlock, but it's gotta be something good if he went through so much trouble to hide it."

A jab of disappointment pricked her pride. "Where did you find these? I swear I searched that place top to bottom."

"Outside. Under the siding."

She slumped back in the chair. "I didn't even look outside. How could I not have thought of that?"

"Melissa showed up. That threw you off. But if it makes you feel better, it was my sister's idea to look under the trailer."

It didn't. She prided herself on completing a job to her best ability. No matter the circumstances. She couldn't let things slip through cracks—couldn't allow herself to make stupid mistakes. Not if she wanted to be taken seriously.

"All done," Amelia yelled, drawing their attention before bounding into the living room and stopping in front of Tommy, hands on hips. "Do you want ice?"

Tommy frowned. "Ice?"

"For your head. Mama always gives me ice for my owies. She takes care of me. I can take care of you."

Tommy grabbed Amelia's little hand, dwarfing it in his own. "That's very thoughtful, but I'll be okay. Besides, you've already done so much. Thank you."

Amelia grinned. "You're welcome."

Pushing to her feet, Sadie handed back the bag. "It's late. We should get going. Are you still up for visiting Clara in the morning?"

Tommy nodded. "You'll have to drive."

She forced a smile. "I'm better at it anyway."

He chuckled, then winced and pressed a hand to his side.

"Are you sure you're okay?" She bit into her lip and debated on the right way to handle this. "I could stay longer. If you need me to."

A slow smile spread across his face. "Maybe you can give me a sponge bath to wash away the dirt?"

"What's a sponge bath?" Amelia asked, bouncing her gaze between Tommy and Sadie.

Tommy tried not to laugh and mouthed *sorry*.

"None of your concern, little one," she said, but not before an image of Tommy glistening in the tub, his rippling muscles exposed for her viewing pleasure invaded her thoughts. Heat roared to life in her belly. Clearing her throat, she rolled her eyes to avoid the mischief dancing in his gaze. She had to get out of here...now. "I'll see you in the morning."

"Bye, Tommy!" Amelia hurled herself against him and gave him a big hug.

Tommy winced but folded his arms around her. "Goodnight, Amelia. Be good for your mom."

Sadie's heart gave a little pitter patter. Amelia had never met her own father and didn't have many men in her life. Seeing her interact so naturally with Tommy stirred something inside her she wasn't sure if she liked, but she recognized the danger.

Her complicated feelings for Tommy were more dangerous than the killer still on the loose. A killer they needed to find fast, or she'd have to spend even more time with a man she needed to stay very far away from.

9

The next morning, every muscle in Tommy's body ached. Sleep hadn't come easy the night before. Partly because of the pain pounding against his head, partly because he'd liked the way Sadie and Amelia looked in his apartment way too much. Having Amelia around softened Sadie, showed a different side of her that Tommy wanted to know more of.

Which scared the hell out of him.

He chanced a peek in her direction as she stood beside him on the small stoop of Clara Parson's home. Her eyes were bright and focused, uniform pressed, and more beautiful than he'd remembered.

Knock it off, Wells.

Refusing to go back down the rabbit hole that had kept him up all night, he focused on the task at hand and knocked on Clara Parson's front door.

She answered with wide, olive-green eyes and her nose scrunched in confusion after only one loud knock. A baby sat high on her hip, and a preschooler circled her legs with his chubby arms.

Clara swung her gaze between him and Sadie. "Can I help you?"

He aimed a grin at each of the kids before settling what he hoped was a reassuring smile on Clara. "Hello, Mrs. Parson. I'm Deputy Wells, and this is Deputy Pennel." He tilted his head toward Sadie. He knew Clara by name but had never spoken to the woman. Recognition might have dawned in her eyes when she'd landed her gaze on him, but it was still best to introduce them both.

"We wondered if we could ask you a few questions," Sadie said from beside him.

The little boy pressed himself tighter against Clara's legs.

"What is this about?" Clara asked.

"Shawn Downs." Tommy didn't know how else to approach asking a woman if she was cheating on her husband with a married man, but he remembered Sadie's advice from the day before. Ripping off the band-aide sometimes was the easiest way.

Clara wet her lips and looked past their shoulders then ran a hand over the baby's dark curls. "Come in." She turned into the house, leaving the door open for them to follow.

Tommy waited for Sadie to enter then stepped in behind her and pushed the door shut.

Clara led the way into the living room and placed the baby in a bouncer. She quickly moved a pile of folded clothes from the sofa and tossed them in a waiting laundry basket. Pushing aside some stray toys, she unhooked her little boy from her knees and settled him in a small chair with cartoons all over the fabric. "Just give me a second. I want to put a show on to distract him. Go ahead and take a seat."

Tommy lowered himself beside Sadie on the floral-patterned couch, ignoring the ache in his bones. Sharp pains pierced his side with every breath. Sadie's thigh brushed against his and images of her and the stupid sponge bath he'd foolishly teased her about slammed against him. He slanted his gaze to her folded hands on her lap.

Soft hands.

Capable hands.

The muscles in his groin tightened. Shit. Every thought of what Sadie's hands could do to him gave him enough of a fit last night. He couldn't let it torture him today. Especially not with a baby sitting in front of him, staring at him with big blue eyes and drool dripping from her mouth.

"Sorry about that." Clara perched on the edge of a chair in front of the large picture window. "It'll be easier with him distracted. What do you want to know about Shawn?"

"I understand you two were in a relationship in high school." Sadie took the lead. "Were the two of you still in contact?"

Clara dropped her gaze to the hands she clenched together on her knees. "We dated a long time ago. A lifetime ago, really."

Tommy leaned forward to hear her quiet voice, nearly swallowed by the singing monkeys on television. "And recently?"

Tears swam in her eyes. "We've talked."

Tommy blew out a long breath. He'd rather walk through a minefield than press Clara on her relationship with Shawn. But it had to be done. "Did he mention anything to you about anyone wanting to hurt him? Was he in an argument with anyone?"

She shook her head. "No." Tears spilled over her cheeks, and she swiped them away.

"I don't mean to be indelicate," Sadie said. "But we have to know. Were you and Shawn romantically involved?"

Clara pressed her fingers against closed eyes. "Oh my God. How did you know? This can't get out. If Mitch knew. If someone told him..."

"We haven't spoken with your husband." Tommy wanted to reassure her that Mitch wouldn't find out what she'd done, but if her husband already knew what his wife was up to, he'd just become suspect number one. "But could it be possible someone else did?"

Dropping her hands, she stared at him with devastation written on every line in her face. "We were so careful. And we only slept together a couple times." She darted her gaze to her children, both facing the large screen with blank eyes.

Gaining his wits, he glanced around the room. A smattering of toys littered the floor, but otherwise not a speck of dust lingered on any surfaces. A light scent of vanilla or cupcakes or something sweet lingered in the air. This was a home, put together by someone who cared about their space. How could a married mother of two who seemed to have her life together end up in bed with Shawn?

God, he hoped it wasn't at Shawn's place. He fought a cringe and shoved the ridiculous thought from his head. This wasn't a time for judgement. Why she made her choices didn't matter—only if those choices were the reason Shawn ended up dead.

A sharp gasp regained his attention. Clara stood and covered her opened mouth with her hand. "How did you know? If you found out, Mitch could have, too. Oh my God. What am I going to do? What if he knows?"

A soft whimper sounded from the baby. Her lip trembled.

Sadie rose and offered a comforting hand to Clara. "We asked the right questions. People talk to us, especially when someone is murdered."

Clara bit into her thumbnail, obviously not convinced her secret was well guarded.

"Now, have you and Shawn been...speaking...for a while?" Sadie asked.

"A few months."

A loud wail came out of the tiny baby, and Tommy cringed.

Clara swooped the child into her arms and bounced up and down. "I was lonely. Mitch and I had a big fight. I ran into

Shawn at the bar. We started talking about old times. It was like the old Shawn was back. He was upset about his situation with Melissa. I thought..." She shrugged and wiped the tears from the baby's face. "I don't know what I thought. Maybe I could have my old life back—a life with someone who really loved me. Maybe we could help each other."

Feeling foolish as the only one still sitting, Tommy stood. "Is there any reason for you to believe Mitch found out about your relationship with Shawn? Has he been short-tempered lately? Angry? Or possibly the opposite. More attentive and loving? Maybe afraid to lose you and trying hard to hold on?"

She snorted. "No way he'd be attentive and loving if he found out I had an affair. Especially with Shawn. And if he knew, trust me, he'd make sure I paid."

Her words were like rocks landing in Tommy's stomach. "What does that mean? Would he hurt you?"

She pressed the baby tight to her chest like a shield.

"Clara. Has Mitch hurt you before?" Sadie pivoted, blocking the boy sitting in front of the television as if she could protect him from the ugliness of the conversation.

"He's a passionate man. Sometimes he can get out of control. It's usually just yelling."

Anger had Tommy fisting his hands. "Usually?"

Clara met his stare, her silence enough to answer the question.

Sonofabitch.

"We should get going." Sadie pressed a card into Clara's palm. "If you think of anything that can help us figure out who killed Shawn, please call. For that, or any other reason. We're here for you. I'm here for you. There are places that can help keep you and your children safe. All you have to do is ask."

Clara sniffed back her emotion. "He wanted to change. Wanted to get his life back on track. Said he needed to make amends before he could bury his demons."

"And he never mentioned what those demons were? Who he needed to make amends to?" Tommy asked.

"I wish he had."

Tommy thanked her for her time then followed Sadie to the car. The delicate situation had just turned downright hazardous. He needed to find out how much Mitch knew without clueing him into his wife's extramarital activities. Clara's safety depended on it.

SADIE CLIMBED behind the wheel of her cruiser. She pinched the bridge of her nose and fought against the growing panic for the woman she'd just met. "We have to talk to her husband. No way we can assume he didn't know about Clara and Shawn. And if he has a temper like his wife described, it's not hard to picture him taking his anger out on Shawn."

Tommy stared out the window, gaze locked on the pretty picture window with frilly curtains framing the inside. The delicate loops of lace visible from the car. "You're right. But I don't see him not taking it out on her. He'd make her pay."

A shudder ripped down Sadie's spine. "If Mitch did kill Shawn because he found out about the affair, then he took away a future with a man she once loved—could have loved again—but that won't be enough. Not for a man like Mitch."

"Let's take a look at his file when we get back to the station. I want to see if there's ever been more than complaints of disorderly conduct by the neighbors."

"Good idea. The more we know about Mitch Parson before we talk to him, the better." Sucking in a breath, she tore away her gaze from the pretty blue house and pulled onto the road. So many memories coming back to attack her—memories of all the scary houses and even scarier men who held control over her mother and her. She wanted better for Clara and her children.

"I also want to see the papers you discovered at Shawn's, and we need to figure out what that key is for." She'd wanted to see them last night but had high-tailed it out of his apartment. When she'd realized she'd forgotten to ask for them, she'd been too big of a chicken to head back upstairs.

"Shit. I forgot the evidence bag at my place. Can you swing by so I can grab it? Sorry. I felt like I'd been hit by a bus when I crawled out of bed. My focus was on getting dressed and out the door on time. The evidence bag with the papers was the last thing on my mind. It'll only take a second."

She cast him a quick glance. The color of the bruise on his cheekbone had deepened to a nasty purple with tinges of green sprouting from the middle, highlighting the scar she'd always wondered about. Bags hung heavy under his eyes. The rest of his injuries couldn't be seen, but she'd noticed how slowly he'd moved all morning. "How do you feel? Any better?"

"Not really. Everything still hurts, but it is what it is."

She understood that mantra. Life went on, time kept moving, no matter what twists and turns came along. Driving through town, she spied a parking spot outside the pizza shop Tommy lived above and slid in along the deserted sidewalk.

Tommy's phone buzzed, and he shifted to pull it out and look at the screen. "Great. Things keep getting better and better."

His exasperation made her give him a hard look. "What's wrong?"

He leaned his head back against the head rest and turned to face her. "Text from my buddy at the autobody shop. My cruiser's totaled."

She grimaced. "That sucks. I'm sorry."

He ran a hand over his face. "I need to stop at my dad's. He's got a spare truck I can use until I get assigned a new cruiser. Do you mind if I run up and grab the stuff then you take me to his place? He lives just outside of town."

"Sure."

Tommy hurried out of the car and disappeared into the brick building beside her.

Huffing out a sigh, Sadie closed her eyes. A million thoughts swam in her brain, each one bringing only more questions and no answers. She made a mental list of everything they needed to accomplish today. Create a plan for interviewing Mitch Parson, dig deeper into the reason Shawn was paying his friend and employer on a monthly basis, and she still had more questions for Melissa Downs and the weird dynamic between her and Shawn. As the list grew longer, the sheer volume of work and shit to wade through weighed down her limbs.

A sharp pounding on her window made her jump. Her eyes flew open. She faced the driver's window and found herself staring into the angry eyes of a man she'd never met. His strong jaw was clenched tight, a vein bulging against his temple.

She rolled down the window. "Can I help you?"

"Yeah, you can help me. You can tell me what you were doing talking to my wife earlier."

Her heart raced, but she couldn't let it show. "And you are?"

He rested one arm on top of the car and leaned forward, pressing his face into the interior. "Don't pretend like you don't know who I am. You were just at my house with that asshole, Wells. How dare you show up when I'm not there, harassing my family."

It took every ounce of will power she possessed not to react to his anger—or his invasion of her personal space. She couldn't show her hand. Not when tipping Mitch off to the real reason they were at his house could be detrimental to Clara's safety. "Sir, Deputy Wells and I are investigating the murder of Shawn Downs. It's important we interview anyone who knew him. Whether recently or in the past."

He slammed the palm of his meaty hand against the car. "Bullshit. My wife hasn't had contact with that piece of shit since high school."

"Sir, aren't you a school teacher? Why aren't you at work?" Her only hope was to distract him, steering him away from the topic of his wife.

He snorted. "Thank God for nosey ass neighbors. I got a call a sheriff's deputy was at my house. The principal sat in on my class so I could see what happened. Imagine my surprise to see you pulling out of my driveway."

"I assure you, sir, it was just part of our investigation. Routine questioning." She shifted her gaze toward Tommy's building. Where was he? It shouldn't take this long to grab a damn bag and get his ass back outside.

"Do you think I'm an idiot?" He pressed his face closer, the blue eyes just like his baby girl's full of venom. "You showed up at my house when you knew I wouldn't be there. Why? What does my wife know? What does she have in this?"

Her gut churned, but she swallowed the anxiety dancing up her esophagus. She'd dealt with bigger pricks than this in her life. No way she'd let him intimidate her. "I suggest you back away and calm down. I'd be more than happy to speak with you about the matter of Shawn Downs, but not like this. Not with you breathing down my neck demanding answers for some perceived slight. Now. Back off."

He sneered. "Or what?"

She clasped her hand on her weapon and pushed at the door. She'd had enough of his bullshit.

"Parson! What the hell do you think you're doing?" Tommy strode over, authority ringing loud in his stern voice.

Mitch took one step back and raised his palms. "Just asking the lady some questions."

"She's not just a lady, she's a deputy and my partner. Go

home or back to work...wherever you need to be right now. We'll schedule an interview later."

Mitch grinned, the anger and hostility sliding off him. "No problem." He retreated to his car with his hands in his pockets, whistling the whole way.

Tommy jumped in beside her. "You good?"

She blew out a long breath. "Yeah. Man, that guy's an ass." She might not have understood why a pretty woman with two small children would risk it all by stepping outside her marriage with a man like Shawn, but she did now. Mitch Parson didn't respect women—his wife or the ones who served the law—but how far would he go to hurt a man who was part of his wife's betrayal?

An image of Shawn's body floated into her mind. Yeah, Mitch was angry enough to hunt down a man and make sure his victim knew exactly who killed him. Only one question remained. Did Mitch know Shawn was sleeping with his wife?

10

Coffee dripped into the now-full pot, the liquid slowing as it finished brewing. Tommy filled two mugs and brought them to the kitchen table. Anger still vibrated his bones after their encounter with Mitch Parson. He needed a second to calm himself before jumping back into action.

"It's so beautiful here." Sadie hooked her fingers around the handle of the mug and slid it closer. She sat with her chin propped in her hand and gaze fixed out the floor to ceiling windows in the adjacent great room.

He took the chair across from her and shifted to enjoy the view. His dad's cabin was tucked into a dense patch of woods. Trees glistened with snow and light flurries fluttered to the forest floor beyond the glass, the mountains visible beyond. He faced her with a grin. "You sound surprised."

She lifted the steaming mug to her mouth, but he'd caught the amused smirk before she took a long sip. "Your dad found a slice of heaven. And with the Christmas tree in the corner and the snow falling outside—it's like a scene from one of those old-time movies. I can only imagine the room with a roaring fire and the lights twinkling from the branches of the tree." With her hands still wrapped around the mug, she set it back on the table.

Tommy couldn't keep his eyes off her. As she talked, the tension melted away from her face. Her full lips curved into a small smile. Her hair was still pulled back into the ponytail she preferred, but a softness he couldn't look away from settled over her features.

She blinked, landing her focus on him, and a light blush pinked her freckled cheeks. Without her usual tough-as-nails attitude wrapped around her, it was easy to see the person she was when she let her guard down. Gentle, nice, and pretty as hell.

"Sorry. We're not here to talk about your dad's cabin or Christmas trees." She traced the pad of her finger over the white rim of the mug.

"We're here to decompress after the incident outside my apartment with Mitch. I can't think straight when I'm upset. No better way to take a breather than sitting and talking about simple things for a minute."

The tense lines of her face hardened again. Dammit. He wanted her soft and easy to talk to. Maybe if he kept her mind off work for just a little while longer. "Where did you live before you came to Water's Edge?"

"Where didn't I live?" she asked with a soft chuckle, her expression growing sad. "My mom had a bad habit of falling for very bad men. She'd fall in love, we'd move, then head to a shelter as soon as things blew up in our faces—which they always did. That's why I'm so passionate about helping at the shelter."

He leaned back against the hard chair. Her upbringing didn't just explain her constant presence at Safe Haven Women's Shelter, but also why she kept her walls up so damn high. She'd been hurt—a lot—and wanted to protect herself and her daughter. "I'm sorry about that, but I know how much you and Amelia mean to Mrs. Collins."

She grinned. "She's the best. And thanks for your sympathies, but my past made me who I am today. Honestly, it's what pushed me into joining the Army as soon as I turned eighteen. And if I'd never done that, I wouldn't have Amelia."

"I didn't know you were in the service. Thank you for that."

Lifting a shoulder, she connected their gazes. "There's a lot most people around here don't know about me."

He cringed. Sure, her tough exterior made it difficult to get close to her—or even want to spend any time with her outside of work. But he should have tried harder. Water's Edge was a small town full of people who chose to stay and live in the same place they grew up. Hell, where their parents grew up. As an outsider, making friends and fitting in couldn't be easy. "I'd like to change that."

She took another sip of coffee. "Why? We weren't friends before this. There's no need to be after."

The hint of hurt in her voice squeezed his insides. Ignoring her comments, he pressed on. "Does your mom live close by? What about siblings?"

Furrowing her brow, she gave him a hard look. "Do you really want to know?"

He nodded.

"Fine." She sighed and tilted her head to the side, as if studying him to figure out why he'd want to know about her family. "I don't have any siblings, and my mom lives in Georgia."

"Are you two close?"

Sadie shrugged. "As close as you can be with someone who constantly questions your decisions."

Tommy chuckled. "I know how that is."

"Really?" She hooked up her mouth in a doubtful smirk.

"Yes, really." He shook his head, not surprised that someone else wouldn't guess how deep his issues with his family flowed. His relationship with his dad might have healed, but he still fought every damn day for people to respect him on his own merits, instead of for who he was related to. And that irritation rubbed his skin raw. "My dad would have done anything to keep Owen and me away from working in law enforcement."

She furrowed her brow. "I figured he'd be thrilled his sons would want to follow in his footsteps."

He snorted out a humorless laugh. "Not at all. He wanted to protect his children like he couldn't protect his wife." He fell silent, the familiar punch in the gut taking his breath away for a moment at the memory of his mom.

Sadie wet her lips and hesitation made her words slow. "You mentioned something yesterday about tragedies. Did you mean the loss of your mother and the trouble with your family?"

The pain in his gut intensified, the pain almost unbearable. He gripped his hands around his mug, concentrating on the warmth seeping into his skin. "My high school girlfriend died in a car accident senior year of high school."

"Oh my God. I'm so sorry." Sadie reached across the table and clasped her hand over his.

Heat spread from her hand and shot to his core. Damn, this was the second time his entire body had reacted to her simple touch. A war waged inside him. Pull away, or let her fingers linger on his skin. His eyes met hers. Her pupils dilated. Her mouth slightly open.

What would she taste like? Would she take control like she did on the job, or would she be like putty in his hands—letting him mold her body in the most delicious ways possible?

The sound of the door opening had him whipping around his head. The muscles in his neck screamed at the sudden movement.

His dad crossed the threshold and kicked off his boots. "What are you two doing here?"

For once, Tommy welcomed his dad's interruption. Clearing his throat, he shifted and pulled his arm from under Sadie's palm. Sure, he'd spent time with women over the years, but he never allowed one to break through his walls. Sadie wasn't some woman he met at a bar—someone to have a good time with then forget about. Hell, he wasn't sure if he'd ever be ready to get past that stage. And even if he was ready to open his heart to another woman, Sadie Pennel was off limits.

SADIE YANKED her arms back across the oak table and rested her hands in her lap. Humiliation scorched her cheeks. She'd let herself get caught up in Tommy's questions and acted completely out of character.

But his confession about his high school girlfriend tugged at her heartstrings, and she'd been drawn to him by some unseen force. The need to comfort him, to show him she cared, was so strong.

She didn't like it—didn't like the tingles of excitement that erupted in her belly when she'd rested her hand on his arm. Or the way he'd looked at her. My God, it was like he wanted to devour her right there on the table like she'd been served to him on a platter.

Okay, the problem was that she liked the way Tommy made her feel way too much.

Sheriff Wells stomped in the kitchen and filled a mug that was sitting beside the ancient coffee machine. Shifting, he leaned against the counter and took a long sip of his drink. His gaze stayed locked on them over the rim of the mug.

She struggled not to squirm.

"My cruiser's totaled. Sadie brought me here so I could grab the keys to the truck you keep parked in the garage."

Sadie.

Her name on his lips tempted a smile. He always referred to her as Deputy Pennel. And as much as him referring to her so casually in front of the sheriff made anxiety pitch in her stomach, the way it sounded made her knees tremble.

The sheriff grunted. "Okay. But that doesn't explain why you're sitting in my kitchen, drinking my coffee, when you should be working."

"Sorry, sir." She sprang to her feet.

Tommy shot her an amused look—sideways grin, deep dimples, laughing eyes.

The sheriff swiped a hand through the air, indicating she should sit back down.

She sat and centered her mind on the series of events that brought them here. The job was her main focus—or should be —and this was a great opportunity to let the county sheriff see that. "We had an unsettling encounter with Mitch Parson in town. We thought we'd take a second to go over things before figuring out the rest of our day. Sorry if we're intruding."

"We're not intruding, right, Dad? He might not admit it, but he loves when we swing by." Tommy winked at her then drained what was left in his mug.

"I usually prefer to be home when you stop by," the sheriff said with a shake of his head and hint of a smile. "But my children are always welcome here. Even when they plan to steal my truck."

Sadie aimed narrowed eyes at Tommy. "You didn't say the truck was your dad's, and you hadn't asked to borrow it."

Tommy shrugged. "What's his is mine, right, Pops?"

"Whatever you say, Son." Sheriff Wells rummaged through a drawer at his side and pulled out a key. Chuckling, he brought the key and his steaming mug to the head of the table and took a seat. He slid the key across the table and into Tommy's waiting hand. "Now, tell me more about what happened with Parson. He's a bad seed. Always has been."

"Bad seed is an understatement. We've had plenty of calls to the station from concerned neighbors. And his wife was pretty clear that he's gotten physical with her." Tommy balled his hands into fists on the table.

Red invaded Sheriff Wells' pale face. "He's hitting his wife?"

The muscles in Sadie's stomach tensed. "Sounds like it. And he's upset we talked to her while he was at work. He seems very controlling. Lacks any respect for women."

"And you spoke to her without her husband there on purpose because?" Sheriff Wells bounced his gaze between the two of them.

"Because she was having an affair with Shawn," Tommy said.

Sheriff Wells whistled low. "Does Mitch know?"

"That's what we need to find out," Sadie said. "As discreetly as possible."

"You said Parson was always a bad seed. Did he get into trouble a lot? I don't remember much about him." Tommy rose to his feet and carried his mug to the sink.

"Your sister would remember him more. He got into quite a bit of trouble when he was younger. Not sure how much of it stuck to his record. But I can tell you one thing, I never expected he'd be the one with a wife, kids, and good job and Shawn the one whose life went down the shitter."

"So Shawn didn't get in trouble with Mitch when they were younger?" Sadie asked, rolling the information around in her head. "Trouble tends to stick together when you're a teenager."

Sheriff Wells scratched the white whiskers on his square jaw. "A touch of trouble here and there, but if memory serves me right, Shawn didn't start butting heads with the law until he went to college. Mitch Parson wasn't around then. He went away to school. Came back after he graduated."

Sadie twisted her lips to the side. "We need to pull Shawn's record. See if there's any correlation between when he started making trouble and anything else he might have gotten mixed up in. Maybe something related to those papers you found. Or even something that triggered him at school." She still needed to take a look at the drawings Tommy had told her about. There could be a picture or date that shook something loose and made sense of everything.

"Agreed."

"Do you have any other leads besides Mitch Parson?"

Tommy nodded. "We have a few angles to dive into. Nothing concrete. Just scratching the surface."

The sheriff folded his arms over his ample middle. "Well, you better start digging deeper."

"We should go." She rose and placed her half-empty mug in the sink next to Tommy's. "Thank you for the coffee, sir."

"Any time. Keep me posted."

She followed Tommy toward the front door, casting one last glance at the jam-packed decorations covering the Christmas tree and the beautiful scenery out the large window. The desire to linger, to go back to the moment she'd shared with Tommy before his dad arrived, slowed each step.

But the moment had passed, the ridiculousness of her response to Tommy shoved away. A new curiosity might be brewing regarding a man she had obviously misjudged, but it didn't matter. She didn't have time to waste wading through his secrets. Like the sheriff said, they had a lot of digging to do. And if they wanted to figure out what happened to Shawn, they'd need a bulldozer to dig through all the wreckage they'd uncovered.

11

The sun broke through the gray clouds. Its bright rays caused the clinging snowflakes on the trees lining the sidewalk to glisten like diamonds. Sadie stopped for a beat in front of the large brick courthouse that stood proud in the middle of the town square. She loved the majestic peaks along the roof and thick columns that flanked the wide double doors. Greenery and boughs of holly lined the archways, matching the festive wreaths on the lampposts dotted around the building.

She'd called Judge Downs this time, not wanting to interrupt her mourning period or catch her off guard. Her admission she was at work today had surprised Sadie, but she couldn't fault the woman for wanting something to take her mind off her grief.

"What are you looking at?" Tommy's shoulder brushed against hers.

She scrunched her nose, uncertain how much she should confide. "The courthouse. It's beautiful. It looks like a scene from a snow globe."

Tommy chuckled. "I guess. I haven't stopped and appreciated this place in a long time. It's just part of the town. Something I've always known."

"Well, maybe you should take the time to appreciate what's around you." She slid a glance his way, and her heart sputtered. Dammit, those hazel eyes of his blazed with heat and swallowed her whole.

"I'm starting to realize that."

She dropped her gaze to the ground. "Good to know. Let's get this over with." She trudged forward and pulled open the heavy door, slipping through and holding the edge for Tommy to follow.

Large black and white marble tiles sprawled in front of her, leading down a wide hallway. "Do you know which office is the judge's?" The only time she'd been in the courthouse was to testify in the court room on the second floor.

"All the way at the end on the right. What did you ask Melissa when you saw her yesterday?"

"The basics. We talked about her strained relationship with Shawn. If she knew of anyone who was upset with Shawn, or if Shawn had a history of making trouble." Discreetly, she shifted her eyes from side to side to take in the high ceilings and gilded lights lining the hall.

Tommy stopped in front of a closed door with a brass nameplate boasting the name Honorable Melissa Downs. He pushed the door open, nodding for her to walk through.

She stepped into a room with plush powder blue carpet and dark mahogany walls. Sleek file cabinets lined the far end of the room, and another door led to what she assumed was Judge Downs' actual office.

A well-dressed woman with a sleek gray bob and glasses perched on the end of her nose sat behind a desk. Her fingers busily typed away with her gaze trained on a large computer screen.

"Good morning, Patsy. How's the prettiest lady in Water's

Edge doing today?" Tommy aimed his lethal smile at the older woman.

Patsy glanced up, fingers still moving, and grinned. "You've always had a sweet tongue, haven't you?" Her lightning quick fingers stopped moving, and she turned her smile to Sadie. "Hello, honey. I don't believe we've met."

Sadie reached over the pin-neat desk and shook Patsy's hand. "I'm Deputy Pennel. Nice to meet you."

With her hand still in Sadie's, Patsy rose and closed the distance between them.

"Patsy's worked as the secretary for every county judge in Water's Edge for the past thirty years." Tommy winked at Patsy. "She's a living legend around here."

"Don't forget to mention I changed your diapers when your mama needed a little help." Patsy squeezed his arm. "She was the nicest woman."

Tommy shifted and gave a little nod. "Is she ready to see us?"

Patsy's bright red lips turned down. "Should be. Just knock first."

Sadie hesitated. If Patsy had worked for Melissa Downs the entire time she'd been in office, she might have some insight on the woman. "So, you've worked for Judge Downs a long time. How's she holding up?"

Patsy eyed the closed door before answering. "She's…fine."

Sadie furrowed her brow. The inflection of her words bordered on disapproving. "I'm sure coming into work today was difficult for her. Maybe jumping into her normal routine helps."

Patsy leaned in closer. "You might be right, dear. But it's just not how things should be done."

The older woman's judgement put a sour taste in Sadie's mouth.

Tommy cupped his hand over the black cardigan covering Patsy's shoulder. "We all grieve differently."

Appreciation squeezed Sadie's chest. So far, her experience with small-town gossip and judgement had been that either people participated in it, or they just let others spew their opinions—no matter how nasty or ill-minded. Tommy's willingness to gently step in and defend a woman who'd lost her spouse—even if their relationship was strange—showed her not everyone turned a blind eye to such things.

Patsy snorted and pointed a finger at the door closing off the judge from their conversation. "That's no heartbroken wife in there. That's a politician acting the part and bothered by the spectacle her husband's death has brought to her doorstep. I understand their marriage hasn't been conventional for a while, but there was love there once. She was really there for Shawn when his mom died. It's a darn shame."

The door to the inner office swung open and Judge Downs filled the frame. A deep frown pulled down her entire face. "There you two are. I was just coming out to ask Patsy to call you. Please, come into my office. I'd like to get this over with."

Sadie licked her dry lips and willed her beating heart to stop racing. Melissa hadn't heard anything. Or at least that's what she told herself as she stepped in and faced the judge.

MELISSA DOWNS GESTURED at the two leather bucket seats in front of her huge desk. "Sit, please."

Tommy let his gaze roam over the books lining the built-in shelves surrounding the window behind the judge's desk before he sat. "Thanks for seeing us."

"Yes," Sadie added. "We hate taking more of your time."

Melissa settled into her chair and leaned her forearms on

the desk, hands folded and face grim. "A necessary thing, I understand. I hope Patsy didn't hold you up too long."

Hooking an ankle over his knee, Tommy chuckled. Patsy had been one of his mother's best friends. It didn't matter if he ran into her in the grocery store or showed up in her office for a meeting with the judge involving a murder investigation, Patsy always talked his ear off. At least this time she'd given him information to chew on. "She's a nice woman. I always have a spare minute for her."

Melissa made a non-committal grunt.

Sadie perched on the edge of her chair. "We'll get down to it."

"Perfect. Do you know who killed my husband?" Her hard gaze bore into Sadie, then turned on Tommy.

"We have some leads." Tommy kept his body language relaxed but his mind sharp. His muscles were still too sore to sit at attention like Sadie, but he stayed tuned to the judge's every word. "We'd like to know if you have any insight on Shawn's friendships with Curtis McLane or Mitch Parson."

The judge's face remained stony. "Not much. They were friends in high school. Mitch was a pain in the ass as a teenager. And Shawn worked for Curtis at the bar. Beyond that, I don't have much else to offer. I didn't start dating Shawn until after high school, so I didn't get to know either of them much. Do you think one of them had something to do with Shawn's murder?"

"We're looking into all angles right now," Sadie said.

"How close are you to pinning this on one of those guys? I'd like this dealt with quickly."

"Like Deputy Pennel said, we're looking into multiple avenues at the moment." Tommy fought not to react to Melissa's words. She was a closed book, claiming not to know much about Shawn's high school friends. Maybe he needed to switch gears. "What about Shawn's time at college? That's about the time you two started dating, correct?"

Melissa sighed. "That's right."

"Can you tell us a little more about your relationship?" Sadie asked.

Melissa squeezed her brown eyes closed for a bit. When she opened them, they were filled with sadness. "Shawn and I bonded over the loss of our mothers. We understood each other's pain. He came home from college one weekend, and we decided to give things a try. Until then he'd been seeing some other girl at school, but it wasn't working. So, two heartbroken kids jumped in with both feet and took a bet on love. We got married fast and separated not long after. For years, I tried to convince him into therapy. Tried to make things work. But the more he turned to the bottle, the less he wanted to do with me."

"What can you tell us about his trust fund?" Sadie asked, stepping in and changing the path again.

"Can you be a little more specific?" Melissa tightened her jaw.

"Most parents who create a trust for their children do so in preparation for the day when both parents are deceased. Either as a way to protect their assets upon passing and transition funds in an easier manner, or to provide for their children if the parents were to tragically pass when the children are young."

Melissa raised her brows. "What's your point?"

"Shawn received an allowance from his trust every month after his mother died until he inherited the entire trust at twenty-five. This isn't common when one parent is still living. Do you know why the trust was set up in this way?"

A beat of silence passed, the ticking of the grandfather clock in the corner echoing off the cherry-paneled walls. Tommy gripped the arms of the chair. The judge never broke eye contact with Sadie, and Tommy had to give it to her, she didn't flinch.

"Shawn's mother established the trust. She came from money, and she wanted to make sure Shawn was always taken care of." Melissa leaned back into her chair. Heat lit her eyes.

She hit a nerve. Tension thickened the air. Tommy straightened. "Were you able to track how Shawn spent the money once it was transferred to him?" He doubted it, but he might as well see if Melissa knew about the payments to Curtis.

"No." The word came out clipped, hard. "Probably wasted it on alcohol. That's all he cared about. Now, is there anything else you need to know? Or can I get on with my day? I have a lot of work to do."

Defensiveness dripped from her pores. No more information would come from her—at least not today.

Tommy shifted his glance to Sadie, who gave an almost imperceptible nod, then rose. "If we have any more questions, we'll reach out. Thank you for seeing us."

Melissa nodded then grabbed a file from the corner of her desk, dismissing them like school children from the principal's office.

Tommy shuffled out the door behind Sadie and waved to Patsy. He didn't have the time or patience for more chit chat. His heavy boots clunked against the marble floors, but he kept his mouth shut until he stepped outside and drew in a deep breath of fresh air. "That was interesting."

Sadie ran her palm over the top of her hair then twined the long strands of her ponytail between her fingers. "Yeah. I'm not sure what to make of it. She was so broken up when I saw her yesterday. Today she seemed less sad and more...inconvenienced."

"Maybe she didn't want to show emotions at work. Keep things professional." Tommy shoved his hands in the warm fleece pockets of his coat.

Sadie turned toward the station and made her way down the sidewalk. "Is Taylor working today?"

Tommy fell into step beside her. "I think so, why?"

"We need to talk to her about Shawn's accounts. Find out who gets all of the money from the trust with him passing since we didn't find a will. Getting a chunk of his inheritance would be a good reason to stay married. We haven't gotten confirmation on who was the holdout for divorce. Maybe Melissa wanted the trust fund and Shawn didn't care enough to push."

Tommy nodded. "We should poke around her accounts if possible. Not sure if we'll be able to secure a subpoena for the county judge. But if she does get the money, we need to make sure she doesn't have any big-time debt or bad habits."

Sadie sucked in a breath. "Did we just put Shawn's wife down on our suspect list?"

A pinch of guilt squeezed his conscience. "Just following the facts."

"True." Sadie might have agreed, but weariness vibrated her voice.

He understood her trepidation. Going down any path that pointed a finger at the judge wasn't one he wanted to travel.

12

A yawn ripped through Tommy's mouth, and he stretched his arms above his head. The motion caused the constant discomfort in his side to morph from a dull annoyance to a stabbing pain. He winced and lowered his arms, taking in the mostly empty desks around him in the main hub of the sheriff's station.

Noises gurgled from his stomach. Lunch had been spent at his desk, eating a sandwich from the vending machine in the waiting room. He'd need to take off soon to make it to Katherine's in time for dinner. She'd tracked him down earlier and insisted he come over. An offer he gladly accepted. Especially if it meant he didn't have to scrounge up food after working all day.

Picking up the file on his desk, he tried to train his focus on the myriad of information he'd uncovered about Mitch Parson. He and Sadie decided to each take a suspect. He looked into Mitch's background. She took Curtis. They'd deal with Melissa Downs together.

He threw the file down. A low buzz fluttered in his brain. He was tired and hungry and there was no way in hell he'd be productive until he gave his eyes a rest. Besides, he'd have to fill Sadie in on what he'd found. No reason to read the same things over again for his benefit only.

He watched her from across the room—the familiar concentration in her scrunched brow and narrowed eyes. She tapped the tip of a pencil against her desk, her nose wrinkled as she studied her computer screen.

Chuckling, he moved toward her. They hadn't talked since arriving at the station after speaking with Melissa than splitting up their assignments. She'd wandered into his mind too many times than he cared to admit. "Find anything good?"

She leaned back in her chair. "Curtis' bar limped along until he started getting money from Shawn. Other than that, the guy's clean. No record. No arrests. Nothing to point at him being shady."

"Except him taking money from his friend and employee."

"Besides that." She pointed the pencil at him. "I called and set up an interview with Curtis tomorrow to talk about the money he took from Shawn. I asked him to come here. Thought it might shake loose more information."

Tommy perched on the corner of her desk. "Good plan."

"I also located Shawn's college roommate and checked into his files with the school. He definitely hit a rough patch, going from model student to troublemaker almost overnight. I tried to uncover any records pertaining to actual legal issues—not college misdeeds—but I couldn't find any."

"Really? My dad remembered him getting into trouble. That should all be documented."

She lifted a shoulder. "Nothing I found."

He'd bring it up to Katherine and Owen tonight. See what their take was. "What about the roommate? Did you speak with him?"

She shook her head. "Not yet. I left a voicemail. Hopefully

he calls back soon. What about you? Find anything to help when we talk with Mitch?"

Crossing his arms, he shrugged. "Plenty to support everything we heard. Has some dings on his record for different physical altercations over the years. A restraining order filed shortly after high school. A girl from college who claimed to date him for a few months, and when she broke things off, he went crazy. Assaulted her and the guy he found her with."

"Based on personality and past issues, Mitch is the one who fits the profile for Shawn's killer. Crime of passion. Payback for his wife stepping out on him and humiliating him for sleeping with the town drunk. I'm sure Clara having an affair with Shawn would hit his ego much harder than if she'd chosen anyone else."

"I agree, but I also don't see him sitting back and not going after Clara. He has a history of abusing women. Of lashing out and not respecting women. My gut says he wouldn't let Clara go unpunished."

Sadie's eyebrows rose to her hairline. "Unpunished?"

"That's how he'd see it, not me." He lifted his palms in surrender.

"We need to talk to him. Soon." She grabbed a piece of paper from her desk drawer and scribbled something down.

He leaned forward for a better view. "What's that? A list?"

"Lists help me focus. Keep me organized."

He read down the numbered lines. "Are these tasks in a certain order?" He chuckled, unable to hide his amusement.

"As a matter of fact, they are." She hoisted the paper in front of his face.

He ran his finger down the lines. "You still haven't looked at the drawings?"

"Next on the list."

He glanced at the time on the bottom corner of Sadie's computer. "You plan to do that tonight?"

She offered him a shy smile. "I thought I'd take them home. Once I put Amelia to bed, I'll have plenty of time to look them over."

"What will you do for dinner?" The question popped out of his mouth before he could think better of asking it.

She shrugged. "Haven't thought much about that yet. After I pick up Amelia from the shelter, I'll probably throw something together. Something quick and easy."

"After such a long day, that sounds like too much work. You and Amelia are going with me to Katherine's for dinner." He dipped his fingers into the front pocket of his pants.

"What?"

"Katherine wants me and Owen to go to her place for dinner. You can come with me, and you can browse through the pictures on the way. Then we can pick her brain. If you're not there, I might forget to ask something important." He pulled his eyebrows together, trying to look solemn.

She rolled her eyes, but a hint of a smile burst on her lips. "You don't want me and my daughter tagging along."

"You're my partner on this. We should be together when talking to key witnesses. Besides, Amelia cracks me up, and she'll probably love spending time with my nephew. He's only a year younger. Plus, Nora will be there, and we both know how much Amelia loves Nora."

"Your sister is a key witness now, huh?" Sadie asked, ignoring all his other bullet points.

"Could be." He grinned, dipping his chin so they were eye-to-eye. "Come on. You don't really want to look at creepy pictures alone in your dark house, do you?"

She pressed her lips together, pulling them to the side. "Are you sure?"

"Wouldn't have brought it up if I wasn't sure."

"Katherine won't mind? I wouldn't want to put her out."

"Not at all. She's a nice person. I bet you'd like getting to know her better."

She finally lifted her eyes to his. Something lingered behind her brown irises—excitement, hope, nervousness? "I'd like that."

He grabbed her coat from her chair and held it open. "Coming to dinner or getting to know Katherine?"

Turning her back, she stuffed her arms in the coat then glanced over her shoulder with a grin. "Both. It'll take me some time to drive to Pine Valley to grab Amelia, and I'd like to head home and change."

"Sure. Forty-five minutes long enough? I'll stop home and change, too. Then I'll pick you up."

She nodded and scooped the evidence bag with Shawn's drawings and her to-do list off her desk. "Perfect."

He watched her walk out the door with her belongings pressed to her chest. No purse, no coy look back to see if his eyes were on her, no presentation of what she thought people wanted to see. She was one hundred percent herself. A deadly combination of badass cop and mysterious woman. A combination he was finding harder and harder to resist.

Sadie placed her fork on her empty plate and pushed it away. Licking every last dribble of the creamy sauce from the chicken pot pie Katherine made was too tempting to keep the dish under her nose.

Much better than the chicken nuggets she'd planned to pop in the oven.

"Ms. Katherine, this pie is yummy. But where's the chocolate?" Amelia asked, her brow wrinkled in confusion.

Marie laughed and mopped a mess of peas and carrots

from Nora's face. "I should have known your mind would go to sugar."

Grinning, Sadie rolled her eyes. "Thank you again for having us over and excusing my silly daughter. I know you didn't plan on feeding two extra mouths."

"No problem at all." Katherine stood and grabbed the pie pan from the center of the table. Her sandy brown hair was tied back in a low ponytail and the dimples in her cheeks mirrored her brother's. She carried the dirty dish to the sink and filled it with sudsy water. "And don't worry, Amelia. I always have chocolate in this house."

Tommy leaned back in his chair and sighed. "What did I do to deserve my favorite dinner tonight? You hate cooking this. Always say it takes too damn long." He winked at the little Amelia, who sat beside him.

"Uncle Tommy said damn, Mommy." Oliver, Katherine's son said with wide brown eyes and a wicked grin.

"Language." Katherine turned and pointed a fork at Tommy. "And after last night, I would have made you anything you wanted. But I knew this was high on your list."

Owen stood and slapped a hand down on Tommy's shoulder. "So that's all we have to do, huh? Almost get hit by a train to get you to spoil us?"

Katherine aimed the fork at Owen. "Get that thought out of your mind right now."

"Thanks for that," Marie said with a snort.

Reaching around the table, Katherine's husband, Theo, gathered the rest of the dirty dishes and piled them in his arms. A well-trimmed, dark beard covered his jaw and blue eyes sparkled behind his black-framed glasses.

Sadie stood to help.

"We got this. Sit back down." Theo smiled and carried the soiled serving ware to the sink.

"Are you sure? Really, I don't mind."

"Trust me. Don't argue." Tommy wrapped an arm around Oliver and hugged him close to his side.

Sadie sank back to the chair with her gaze locked on him. Since they'd stepped foot in the house, Oliver had been glued to his side. And she wasn't sure which one of them enjoyed it more. The carefree attitude he'd shed while on the job came back in full force around his nephew. His laugh was contagious, and the little guy was cute as a button, his shy smiles coaxing Amelia into playing before they sat for dinner.

She glanced at the sink, where Theo slapped Katherine's butt and Katherine laughed while dotting his nose with suds. A pinch of envy turned her away. After Amelia's father had been killed overseas, she'd never wanted another man.

Never trusted another man.

But the picture-perfect family moment was one Sadie wanted more than she'd ever realized.

"I'll let most of this soak." Katherine returned to the table and sat next to her. "Theo and Marie, can you take the kids in the living room for a few minutes?"

Oliver aimed worried eyes and a deep frown at Katherine. "Is something wrong?"

Katherine smiled. "Not at all. I just need to talk to Uncle Tommy, Uncle Owen, and Sadie for a second alone. We'll call you in when we're done. Why don't you draw a picture for Amelia? I'm sure she'd love to see what an amazing artist you are."

Oliver's frown transformed into a beaming smile. "Okay. Do you like cats?"

"I love them! I have one at my house. A big orange tabby named Mittens." Pride puffed Amelia's little chest as she spoke of their treasured pet.

Oliver wrinkled his brow, tilting his head to the side. "Mittens?"

Sadie laughed at his dubious expression. "His paws look like he has on little white mittens."

Oliver giggled. "I'll draw a picture of him." He jumped off his seat and ran into the other room.

Amelia hesitated. "What should I draw?"

"Hmm," Tommy said, rubbing his index finger over his chin. "Can you draw me a rainbow?"

"I love rainbows!" Amelia squealed as if the two had discovered a deep-seated secret. "I'll make the prettiest one ever."

Marie snagged Nora from her highchair and rested her on her hip. "Can Nora help you pick out the colors?"

"Yes! Let's go." Amelia disappeared in a flash, the sound of animated chatter between the two children quickly floating into the kitchen.

"I'll keep them busy while you guys talk." Theo stood behind Katherine with his hands on her shoulders. "It was nice to see you, Sadie."

"You, too." She watched Theo kiss the top of Katherine's head and walk out of the kitchen. A sinking feeling in her stomach had her dropping her gaze. She'd never been one of those girls who longed for a man. Never needed a boyfriend to make her happy. But seeing the love—and hell, the fun—between Katherine and Theo made something shift inside her. Something she wasn't so sure she wanted to acknowledge.

"So." Katherine wiped a few stray crumbs onto the floor. "What do you two want to know? You've worked the case for two days now. I'm not sure what I can add."

Owen poured a mug of black coffee and settled back at the table.

"We're curious about Shawn's dynamics with Curtis McLane and Mitch Parson. Mostly in high school, but if you have any knowledge of their relationships recently, we'd like to hear that, too." All traces of Tommy's good nature slipped away.

Katherine ran her hand over her smooth ponytail. "I didn't

know much about them then or now. I remember Mitch always causing problems at school. Suspensions, detentions, and everything in between. Shawn and Curtis seemed like nice guys. The three were always together, but those two seemed to be closer. Not really caring if Mitch was around."

"Do you remember when Shawn's behavior shifted?" Sadie asked.

Katherine settled her hands in her lap and rested a gentle gaze on Tommy. "I do remember. He was at school, but he came home every weekend to visit his mom. She had cancer, and I'd heard talk it was hard for him to be away. But it was after our mom died that he started causing trouble when he came back to town. That's why it stands out so clearly in my mind."

Sadie chanced a peek at Tommy, who sat back and rubbed a hand over his mouth, then shifted in her chair to face Katherine. "Tommy told me about your mother. I'm sorry you had to go through that. But I have to ask. What kind of trouble did Shawn cause?"

Katherine blew out a long a breath and wiped away moisture at the corners of her eyes.

Owen rested a hand over hers and squeezed. "He stole a car. Broke into the liquor store. Threw rocks at people's houses, causing a ton of damage. He scratched the hell out of his dad's sports car. Then he was too drunk to do much besides pass out all over town. At first, people were relieved to see him drinking because he wasn't harming anything else but himself. I was new on force back then. We got almost daily calls."

"I didn't see any of that when I searched for his files." Had she missed something? If Owen was right about all the issues Shawn had, she should have found his criminal record.

"Really? That's weird." Owen furrowed his brow. "Maybe there's a glitch in the system or something. The courthouse stores a ton of paper files in the basement. You should be able to search down there and find them. It's not the most sophisticated back-up system, but it's better than nothing."

Sadie's mind went back to the drawings she'd glanced through on the way over. "Was Shawn artistic in school?"

"Yes, very." Katherine said, nodding. "Why?"

"I found pictures he drew—along with a random key—stuffed in between the siding of his trailer the night I went over there," Tommy said. "Creepy stuff."

"You mentioned he stole a car and keyed his dad's car. He drew a lot of pictures of car crashes, burning cars, one picture was of a vehicle running over his dad."

Katherine pressed a hand to her chest. "That sounds crazy."

"Could be random thoughts and ideas. Could be a look into something deeper going on in his life. Something pushed him to his breaking point." Sadie's phone rang in her pocket, and she retrieved the cell. She didn't recognize the number, but the area code was local. "Sorry. I should take this."

"No problem," Katherine said.

Sadie hit the Answer button. "Hello."

"Help! I need help, now! Please. You have to stop him. He's lost his mind." The woman's frantic pleas pierced her eardrum.

Sadie locked her gaze with Tommy. She might not have recognized the number, but she recognized the voice. "Clara. What's going on? I need to know what's happening. Where are you?"

"My house. He came home in a rage. Please. Hurry!"

Tommy shot to his feet. "Is she in trouble?"

Sadie lifted a finger then mouthed, "Call dispatch. Get a car to the Parsons' now."

"He knows what I did. He won't let me leave. My babies. He has my babies." Clara's ragged sobs tore through the line and sent shock waves around Sadie's heart.

"Stay on the phone. I'm coming."

13

Sadie tapped the tip of her toe against the floor of Tommy's truck as he screeched to a stop in front of the Parsons' house. Thank God Marie was at Katherine's house, and she could leave Amelia with zero worries, allowing her to focus solely on the job.

Two squad cars, lights blazing, blocked the driveway. The moon shone through the dark clouds. Three shadowy figures stood in the yard. She strained against her seatbelt to get a better view.

"I'm here, Clara," Sadie said into the phone. "Tommy and I just pulled up."

Putting the car in park, Tommy shut off the engine.

Sadie jumped out and cut through the yard, stomping through the light dusting of snow clinging to the ground. She closed the distance to Clara, who fell against her with tears coursing down her face. Sadie wrapped her arms around the trembling woman. "It's going to be okay."

"He locked me out. I need to get in. I need to get my babies. He got out his gun."

Fatigue and a quiet fear had replaced the frantic pleas.

Clara had stayed on the line as Sadie and Tommy raced into town, but the woman had barely spoken. Too consumed with the unfolding horror to keep Sadie filled in on what was happening.

"Where's Mitch?" Tommy demanded.

"Inside." Brian Sterling, a weathered deputy, dipped his head toward the house. "He has both kids with him."

Pivoting, she faced the house, but cupped her hands over Clara's bony shoulders.

Clara kept her eyes locked on the house, the phone dangling at her side in a loose grip.

"Can you look at me?"

Clara slowly shifted her attention to Sadie. An ugly bruise circled her eye and blood dripped from the corner of her split lip.

A muttered curse sounded behind Sadie, but she couldn't let herself spout off her own opinions. "Did Mitch hit you?' The answer was glaringly obvious, but she had to ask.

"Yes."

"What about the kids? Has he ever hit them before?" She held her breath. As bad as the situation was, maybe Mitch had a soft spot for his children.

Clara shook her head, her focus going back to the pretty picture window with the frilly curtains blocking whatever was going on inside. Tremors shook her body.

Sadie slipped out of her coat and covered Clara's shoulders.

Tommy flicked his wrist toward the house. "We can't just stand here and watch. Someone needs to get inside."

"We know that," the second deputy said.

Sadie squinted through the darkness but didn't recognize the younger man. "What happened when you knocked?"

"Not a damn thing," Brian said. "He refused to answer the door, wouldn't pick up his phone when we called. We can't just use a battering ram and force our way in when he has the kids in there."

"How do you know he's still inside?" Tommy asked.

Brian shot him a hard look. "We have a deputy stationed in the back. No one's been outside. We were here when he shoved his wife out the front. He has nowhere to run."

"Maybe he'll talk to us." Sadie connected her gaze with Tommy above Clara's head. "We're the ones he was upset with. Maybe that's enough to get him to at least let one of us inside to talk him off whatever ledge he's on."

"It's worth a try," Tommy said.

Clara clung to Sadie's arm. "Get my babies. Please. I've never seen Mitch like this before. Never seen him so upset. I don't know how he found out, but he did. He knows what I did with Shawn."

Sadie covered Clara's freezing hand with her own. "We will do everything we can to keep your children safe."

Sadie stepped beside Tommy, the sturdy brush of his shoulder calming the nerves skittering like drunken ants in her stomach. If Mitch hurt the kids because they'd talked to Clara about her affair with Shawn, she'd never forgive herself.

Tommy lifted his fist to knock on the door, stopping mid-air. "Are you ready?"

"Yes." It might be a lie, but she'd never be more ready than now. And the longer they waited, the higher the chances this situation got even uglier.

Tommy knocked.

Nothing.

He knocked again, this time rapping his knuckles against the screen door twice.

Nothing.

Sadie held her breath, straining her ears to hear any type of movement from inside.

Turing his fist, Tommy banged on the door three times.

The piercing cry of a baby gripped Sadie's gut. Every instinct in her body screamed to get in the house and get the kids.

The heavy door swung open, but the screen door remained secured between her and Tommy and Mitch Parson. His face pinched in anger with the baby held in front of his chest. "What the hell do you want? Get off my property. And tell that whore to go, too. She doesn't deserve any sympathy, and she's definitely not getting her hands on these stupid kids."

The baby's wails grew louder, fat tears streaming down her face.

"I had this one asleep until you slammed your stupid fist against the door. Now they're both awake and crying. Damn kids. They just need to shut the fuck up." Mitch gave one shake to the baby.

Sadie fisted her hands at her sides so she wouldn't tear open the door and grab the kid from Mitch's arms. "I'm pretty good with kids. I can take her and try to quiet her down for you."

Mitch glared at her. "Like I'd trust my kid to another dumb bitch."

A wave of his breath slid across her face—warm, stale, and reeking of alcohol.

"Mama!" The toddler charged forward, and Mitch swatted out his hand, sending the small boy backward.

Sadie ran her tongue over her top teeth to keep her words inside. She yearned to grab her weapon and take this idiot out. But he held a baby in his hands.

"Mitch, let's just talk. Man to man." Tommy raised his palms. "I'm sure this is all a big misunderstanding. You don't want to hurt the kids, and we don't want to hurt you. Let's just calm down and figure out how to fix this."

Mitch peered around them to the scene unfolding on his lawn. The shadows hid the details of his face, but the tapping of his toe against the ground and the darting of his eyes told Sadie he was scared. And scared men who felt trapped acted impulsively.

Unlocking the screen door, Mitch pushed it open a crack. "Fine. Wells, you can come in. But don't try anything stupid. I'd hate to take my frustration out on one these screaming brats."

Tommy turned to the side and slid into the house, both doors closing behind him.

Heart pumping, Sadie ran back to the group in the yard. The sheriff had arrived and was speaking with a group of deputies. Clara stood on the fringe, her arms folded around herself, focus fixed on the house.

"He let Tommy in?" The moon wasn't bright enough to show his facial expression, but the sheriff couldn't keep the hint of worry from his voice.

"Yes. He's unhinged and drunk. I tried to talk him into letting me get the kids, but he refused. He had the baby against his chest. If we'd made the wrong move, he could have hurt the kid."

"Oh God." Clara pressed a hand over her mouth. "It's all my fault. If he hurts them, I won't be able to live with myself."

"None of this is your fault," Sadie said.

"Tommy can't do much in there if the guy is using the kids as a shield…or a threat for him to keep his distance," Mike said.

"Agreed," Brian said. "That's the same reason we can't send the SWAT team in with guns blazing. Too risky."

"Are there any other ways into the house?" Sadie asked Clara. "A backdoor left unlocked? A window open?"

"The kitchen door is locked. I already checked. But sometimes Mitch opens our bedroom window a crack. He likes it cold when he's sleeping."

"Where's your bedroom located?" Sadie studied the house. The windows on the ranch level home were all low enough for her to climb into.

"The window is at the back. All the way on the left."

"What are you thinking, Deputy?" Mike asked.

"From the quick look I got, Mitch is with the kids in the front living room. If the window's open, I can sneak inside, creep down the hall, and have the element of surprise."

Mike ran a hand over the back of his neck, gaze darting to the house then back to Sadie. "And what do you plan to do with that surprise?"

"Whatever I have to."

"Wait," Brian cut in. "If we think we might need a tactical shooter, we need to call in the SWAT team. We can't risk the safety of these kids."

Sadie clenched her jaw. "We don't have time to spare. I'm here now, and I'm just as good of a shot as anyone else you have." She stood with shoulders back and chin lifted, daring the deputy to say otherwise.

"Don't take any unnecessary risks," the sheriff said. "Get in and out as soon as possible. You are in no way to endanger the lives of those children. Do you understand?"

"Yes, sir." She grabbed the Glock from her harness and checked the barrel. She was locked, loaded, and ready to go.

With a nod, she jogged toward the back of the house. *Please God. Let this stupid window be unlocked.*

THE DOOR banged shut behind Tommy. He stood, taking in the scene—turned over chairs in the kitchen, kids crying in the living room, a hole punched through the drywall in the hallway.

Mitch took steps backward and sank into the recliner with the baby still pressed to his chest. Her ear-piercing wails had dimmed to a quiet whimper. The boy howled in the corner, his back to them.

The wheels in Tommy's brain raced. How in the world could he get both kids away from their pissed-off father? He took a step forward, his gaze locked on Mitch's face.

"Not an inch closer." Mitch dropped a hand to the side of the chair that sat against the wall. He yanked it back up and rested a gun on his lap.

A cold sweat broke out on Tommy's neck. "There's no need for that." He tipped his head, indicating the revolver.

Mitch cocked his head to the side. "That's up to me. It's my house. My kids. My fucking decision what there's a need for. Maybe if I'd been more forceful, clearer of my expectations, my wife would have stayed home where she belonged."

Licking his lips, Tommy pivoted so he was standing in front of the crying toddler. "You're not going to hurt your kids. Hell, you're not going to shoot me, either. Not with a yard full of cops on your lawn."

Mitch's gaze flicked to the window then back to Tommy. "It'd serve her right. She thinks she can embarrass me in my town? Run around and spread her legs for some drunk? I'll make her pay. I'll take away what she loves most."

Bile churned in Tommy's stomach. "You don't mean that. I understand you're upset. But you don't have to take things so far. You don't want to be with Clara anymore, fine. Kick her out. Leave her. Whatever. But don't do something we both know you'll regret."

A wicked grin split Mitch's face. "I wouldn't regret hurting you. You brought this to my doorstep. I couldn't let it go—had to know what she did to bring you here. It didn't take much for Curtis to spill everything."

Tommy silently cursed himself for not betting on Mitch running to his old pal to find out what he knew. He and Sadie had told Mitch they were speaking with anyone who knew Shawn—that would have included Curtis. "I talked to Curtis. He didn't tell me Clara was having an affair with Shawn."

Mitch grunted. "You think he told you everything, Wells? You're a naïve little dipshit. Running around town like you're some big bad cop. Everyone knows you aren't shit. You're just pretending to be like your asshole dad and brother."

Tommy fumed, but he couldn't respond to the taunt.

"My God, shut that kid up." Mitch kicked out a foot in the direction of his crying son.

"Why don't you let me take him outside? He's just in the way. And you have your hands full with the baby." Tommy held his breath. If he could get one of the children out safely, it'd be easier to concentrate on how to get to the other one.

"You think I'm an idiot?" Mitch barked, making the baby in his arms shudder.

A shimmer of movement caught Tommy's eye. He didn't react—didn't want to clue Mitch into whatever was going on in the hallway. Mitch's chair was wedged in a corner facing the window, an archway to the hall on one side and the dinning room on the other. He wouldn't be able to see what was happening anywhere except right in front of him unless he moved.

Tommy chanced a glance toward the hall. Sadie tiptoed through the darkness. She pressed a finger to her lips, and he casually shifted his focus back to Mitch. "What if he goes to his room? He's what, two, three? He can get back there by himself, and we can keep talking."

Training his glare on the boy, Mitch twisted his lips. "Get your ass back to your room, Davey. I can't listen to you anymore."

Davey cast huge green eyes at Tommy. His round face was red from crying.

Tommy forced a smile on his face and whispered, "Go ahead. It's okay."

Davey ran around the corner.

Tommy didn't chance a peek. He didn't want to give

anything away. He forced a laugh. "Man, so much quieter without the screaming kid."

"Welcome to my life. It's always loud as hell in here. One of them is always crying, Clara's always scurrying around. It's a fucking nightmare." Mitch closed his eyes and pinched the bridge of his nose, the arm wrapped around the baby pulling her closer.

She wailed and squirmed against the confining hold.

"Dammit," Mitch roared.

"I can put her in her bed." Tommy took a tentative step forward. "She has to have a crib or something, right?"

Mitch gripped the gun on his lap. "Stop moving! I need to think. I can't think with all this noise."

A shadow shifted in the corner of his eye.

Sadie.

He'd give his right arm to know what was going through her mind—to talk and come up with a plan. Instead, he was standing helplessly in front of a man whose anger grew by the second. Time was ticking, and he couldn't see a way out of the house that didn't involve someone getting seriously injured. And if Mitch was the only one at risk, he'd take those chances any day. But not with the baby's safety on the line.

He had to keep Mitch's attention on him. "What do you need to think about? Let me help you."

Mitch darted his gaze between Tommy and the window and back again. Understanding lit through the drunken haze in his eyes. "Shit. Shit. Shit! She ruined everything. She brought me to this, and now I'm fucked."

Anxiety tightened his chest. Mitch was close to losing it. Tommy could feel it in his bones.

The sound of feet shuffling caught his attention, and Tommy glanced toward the hall. Sadie gave a brief nod. Panic shot through his veins. What was she doing? He didn't understand what a stupid head-nod in a dark hallway meant.

A loud *thump* sounded from the dining room.

Mitch shot to his feet. The gun dangled at his side. He shifted the baby to his hip and swung toward the noise. "What the hell?"

Tommy lunged forward. Taking Mitch by surprise, he secured the baby in his arms and turned his back to Mitch. If Mitch got off a shot, at least his body would protect the baby and the Kevlar vest under his shirt would protect him.

Gunfire pierced the air as Tommy cradled the baby closer to his body and ran for the door. *Bang!*

"Sonofabitch!" Mitch screamed.

Tommy glanced behind his shoulder as he reached for the handle. Mitch sprawled on the floor, blood oozing from his leg.

Sadie stood above him, kicked the gun from his reach, then pinned Mitch to the ground with her knee between his shoulder blades. She slapped handcuffs on Mitch as Tommy opened the door. "He's down. The kids are fine. Mitch needs an ambulance."

Clara rushed forward and grabbed the baby. "Where's Davey?"

"In his bedroom. He's okay, but probably scared."

Clara ran past him.

Relief stole his breath and adrenaline leaked from his limbs. He locked eyes with Sadie as she rose, the sexy black leather boot she'd worn to dinner still pressed on Mitch's back. He wouldn't have been able to do any of this without her.

Gratitude spread through him. She was his partner, and finally, he was damn glad about that.

14

Sadie's hand trembled as she tried to fit the key into the lock. She'd ridden the high of adrenaline and satisfaction that Mitch was locked away in jail through the last hour or so. But now that the statements were taken and the job behind her, she couldn't steady her fingers to unlock the damn door and get inside.

The extra weight of a sleeping Amelia in her arms didn't help. How could such a small child weigh so much?

"Do you need help?" Tommy's husky voice combined with the whipping wind and slid against the back of her neck.

She gritted her teeth and finally fit the key in the hole. "You didn't need to walk me to my door. I'm fine."

Tommy snorted. "I remember having this same conversation with you last night. Only the roles were reversed."

She cast a grin over her shoulder then pushed open the door. She plunked her keys into the white ceramic dish on a table pressed against the wall. "Mission accomplished. Now to get this little one settled in her bed. Give me a minute."

Tommy stood hunched with his hands in the front pockets of his jeans. The porch light washed over him. Hard lines dominated his face. Creases at the corners of his eyes spoke of more than concern over seeing her to her house. "Take your time."

She tucked in her lips, debating her next move. She didn't want him to take off as soon as Amelia was tucked in for the night. Not after what they'd just been through. "Why don't you grab us a couple of beers from the fridge, and I'll meet you in the living room?"

"Perfect."

She hurried down the carpeted hall to Amelia's room. She kept the lights off and didn't bother to change Amelia into pajamas. Her heart shot to her throat as she stared down at her beautiful daughter. Her entire life was centered around making sure Amelia was safe and loved and happy. The idea that someone would ever hurt one hair on her head twisted her stomach in knots.

Clara Parson had lived Sadie's worst nightmare tonight. Every ounce of her wanted to make sure Clara never had to experience the pain and terror she'd survived tonight, but she couldn't make decisions for anyone but herself. Couldn't force Clara to grab her children and run like hell from the man who hurt her.

Blowing out a shuddering breath, she pressed a kiss to Amelia's forehead and shut her bedroom door as she made her way back out to the living room. Tonight had conjured up too many of her own fears, brought back too many memories she'd tried to bury.

That beer was calling her name.

Tommy sat on the far end of the sectional. He'd draped his jacket over the back of the couch. Mittens sat on his lap, begging for attention. Tommy ran a hand over the fat cat's back. "What do you feed this thing? He's huge."

She settled beside him on the couch and grabbed the brown bottle he'd uncapped and placed on the coffee table. "He may or may not be a little spoiled."

"So full-sized salmon for dinner then?" Tommy scratched the purring cat behind his ears. He lifted his beer and pointed the mouth of the bottle in her direction. "You did a hell of a good job tonight."

His praise warmed the cold place in the pit of her stomach that hadn't thawed since she'd gotten the call earlier from Clara. "I did what I had to. Thank God it was enough." She clinked their bottles together then took a swig.

Tommy drank from the bottle then set it on the stand beside the couch. "Damn, I've never been in a situation like that —never had a kid look at me with terror-filled eyes." He rubbed a palm over his face.

She took another drink and let the cold, bitter liquid coat her dry throat. Unlike Tommy, this hadn't been her first experience dealing with a dangerous situation where kids were involved. Her mind traveled back to another time, another child, another life-and-death situation that had ended in tragedy.

He rested his forearms on his knees. "You were so calm, so in charge. I didn't know what the hell to do until you showed up in the hallway. You're one hell of a cop."

Unshed tears burned her eyes at his compliment. She blinked, hoping they'd evaporate before he noticed them. "Thanks."

He scooted closer. "Are you okay?"

She shook her head, hating that she couldn't keep her emotions in check. "I'm all right."

"Everything's fine. Mitch will go to prison. Clara and the kids are safe."

Squeezing her eyes shut, she tried to block out the memories that assaulted her. Trembling overtook her body.

Tommy took the bottle from her closed fist and strong arms wrapped around her. She tightened her muscles for a beat then melted against him. The tears came faster, harder. Dammit, she had to pull herself together.

A steady hand moved up and down her spine. She concentrated on her breathing, pulling air in slowly through her nose. Opening her eyes, she focused on the green material of his soft sweater. Her rapid heart rate slowed—the tremors stopped.

Embarrassment swept in and took the place of the anguish. Sniffing, she straightened and wiped at her eyes. "I'm sorry. I didn't mean to break down."

Concern shone from his eyes. He kept his large hand locked on her arm. "This isn't about what happened tonight, is it?"

She picked up her beer and drained half of it. She shifted and tucked one foot under her. "Tonight wasn't my first time to see a child so afraid. To fear for his life and hope I could be the person to wipe away all the terror and put him back safely in the arms of his mother." She picked at the moist label on her bottle. Mittens hopped over to her lap and curled into a ball.

Tommy slid his hand down from her arm to rest on her knee. "You don't have to talk about it if you don't want."

Rubbing her fingers through her cat's silky fur helped calm her nerves. She weighed her choices. She could gloss over what had happened in Iraq, hell she could not tell him anything and he'd respect her decision, but what good had keeping everything locked inside done?

None.

She'd pushed every dark secret she'd carried home from overseas deep down into her soul. Her walls stood high, not wanting anyone to witness the ugliness lingering there. And because of that, she kept most people at a distance.

Realization struck her like a blow to the stomach. She trusted Tommy. More than just as a partner she was working a case with, but as a friend...and possibly more. Her chest tightened, and she absently rubbed at her sternum. If she was going to dive in, she might as well tell him all of it. "I never wanted to leave the military. My plan was to be a lifer. Being a part of the Army was the first time I had a real home, a real community and purpose."

Tommy hitched up the corner of his mouth. "I understand that. I've never wanted to be anything but a police officer. Some say it's in the blood."

"I believe that." A sad smile lifted her lips as all her experiences and achievements burst forth in her mind. She'd loved her job, and she'd loved knowing she was making a huge difference.

But then everything changed.

Her mouth dipped into a frown, and she dropped her gaze to her lap. She set her beer on the coffee table.

Tommy gently squeezed her knee. "What happened to make you leave? To make you move here where you didn't know a single person?"

Moisture filled her eyes again, but this time she didn't fight the misting that blurred her vision. "I was stationed in a small town in Iraq. I was a translator. My commanding officer thought the women would trust me more than the men in my unit. My job was to try and gain information we needed for our missions in exchange for giving the women of the village what they needed to survive." She sucked in a deep breath, needing a moment to compose herself. She rubbed her hand over Mittens' exposed stomach, focusing on the feel of the soft fur against her skin—the warmth of his fat little body on her. She couldn't get sucked up in the past. She could tell the story of what happened without being completely transported back there.

"I can understand why your CO would think women would trust you. You're good with people when you want to be." He grinned, his dimples flashing.

She swatted at his chest, and he captured her hand and held it against him. Warmth shot all the way to her toes. Her initial instinct told her to pull away, avoid contact, but the feel of her hand in his comforted her in a way she'd never experienced—in a way she'd never imagined possible.

The humor vanished from his handsome face. "Keep going. If you want. I'm here to listen."

She swallowed, her mouth as dry as the desert she'd spent so much time in. "Most of the time, the information I gathered from the villagers would help lead us to a militia camp or give us inside intel. But once in a while, they'd help us locate dangerous men. Men who had hurt and killed and took no prisoners. If we could get to them before they got to us, everyone was safer."

His thumb moved against the side of her hand. "Sounds like a win-win for everyone."

"It was supposed to be." A weight crushed her lungs, making it hard to breath, but she pushed on. "But then something happened. Something that changed everything."

Keeping their fingers locked, he lifted his free hand and tucked it under her chin. He forced her eyes to meet his. "You don't have to tell me if you don't want—if it's too difficult."

"There was a woman in town who came to me. A man we'd been after for a long time was nearby, but we couldn't pin him down. She agreed to help if we gave her food for her child—her little boy." Tears streamed over her cheeks. Pressure built in her sinuses. But she had to get it all out. "I went to her house to bring her the food. Once I was inside, someone locked the door and set the place on fire. It was a tiny hut. Flames took over the space in seconds. I scrambled to find a way to escape—to get the three of us out. The smoke was so thick. The only way out was through the door. I banged my shoulder against it over and over and over. Even after the flames beat against my skin. Amelia's father finally got to us. I'm the only one who made it out alive. The smoke..." She could still taste the thick smoke, still smell the burning wood and feel the ash-filled air on her lungs.

"I'm so sorry. But you did everything you could."

She shook her head. "I should have done more, been faster. I can still hear their screams, see the terror on their faces as we searched for an escape. I can see Amelia's father's face as he found me and carried me out of there then fell to the ground, never to get up again. I'll never get that moment out of my head. I was supposed to protect them. *He* was supposed to be here to help me raise our daughter." The shaking started again, first her foot tapping then up her leg and torso until it overtook her entire body.

Tommy folded her into his arms again. He pushed stray wisps of hair off her face, his palm lingering on the back of her head. "Come here. You're okay. I've got you."

She buried her face in his shoulder. Sobs caught in her throat. Her heart shattered all over again—for the lives lost and the part she played in it. For the future she'd been robbed of.

He rubbed his palm in a circle between her shoulder blades. "So you left the service because of the trauma?"

"Partly. My back was burned pretty bad. I spent time in the hospital before I was discharged. It's a miracle I didn't lose Amelia. After that, I knew I had to do whatever it took to keep her safe."

His hand flew away from her shoulders. "Oh my God. Am I hurting you?" Concern filled his voice.

She lifted her head, their faces so close together. She offered him a weak smile. "The wounds healed a long time ago. The physical ones anyway. Scars are left behind, but I can't see them, so I forget they're there most of the time."

The tips of his fingers skimmed a jagged scar slashed along his cheekbone. "I understand a little something about scars."

She lifted her hand and grazed her knuckles against the side of his face. "I've always wondered where that came from."

"A story for another time. I promise." He folded her hand in his, halting the motion against his smooth skin. "Are you all right?"

She shrugged. "As all right as I can be. Tonight was tough anyway, but combined with everything from my past... I just needed to let it out. Thank you for being here."

"Thanks for letting me in the door." He held her gaze. Heat shot from his eyes, scorching her core.

She smiled. "I don't think I had much of a choice."

He chuckled. "I know the feeling."

His amusement fled, leaving a look of longing and vulnerability that almost had her pulling away. His warm breath touched her cheeks, his mouth so close she could almost imagine the taste of his lips.

As if reading her mind, his gaze lowered to her mouth.

She traced her lips with her tongue. Her heart fluttered, her breath coming out thready and fast.

Tommy brought the pad of his thumb to her chin, tilting it upward.

She closed her eyes, her breath caught in her throat.

His lips met hers, soft and sweet.

She circled her arms around his neck and brought him closer. His scent—a burst of citrus and pine—invaded her senses. His tongue dipped between her lips, and she opened her mouth on a moan.

The cat meowed and dug his back claws into her legs as he jumped from her lap.

Sadie winced and pulled away, breaking the magic of the moment. Shallow pants escaped barely parted lips. She pressed the back of her hand to her mouth and tried to process what had just happened. She'd just kissed Tommy.

No, she'd just kissed her partner and fellow sheriff's deputy.

She jumped to her feet and crossed her arms over her heaving chest. She couldn't let this happen—couldn't let him walk into her home and tear down her walls and just fall into bed with him. She was upset and vulnerable and nothing more.

"Sadie?" He slowly rose to his feet, confusion plain as day on his scrunched-up face.

She held up a hand and shook her head. "No. This can't happen. It'd ruin everything I've worked for."

Tommy shoved a hand through his hair, leaving it sticking up at the ends. "What the hell does that mean?"

"We work together. Hell, we just started getting along. I'm not going to sleep with you because you listened to my problems."

Fire smoldered in his eyes, and not the kind that made her toes curl. This heat made her want to take a step in retreat. But she held her ground.

"You think I sat here listening to you cry, wanting to know your story, then kissed you to get you into bed?" Hurt bled into his voice and made her cringe.

"That's not what I said. It's just that...this whole thing is coming out of nowhere. I don't know what to make of it." Confusion pounded against her skull.

"Maybe for once the right thing is to stop pushing people away and just accept the fact someone is there for you."

His words hit her heart so hard, they almost knocked the wind from her lungs. "I don't know what to say."

"You've said enough." He grabbed his jacket from the back of the couch and stormed out the door.

She stared after him, the words she wanted to yell lodged in her throat.

15

Tommy woke with a splitting headache and a bad attitude. Neither had left by the time he reached the station. He'd stepped into Sadie's house the night before hoping to find some comfort, a little companionship with someone who'd just witnessed the same horror he had. Instead, he'd listened to her—something he was more than happy to do—and done the worst thing possible.

He'd kissed her.

Guilt gnawed at his conscience even as anger beat along with the pounding in his skull. Never in his life had a woman accused him of just trying to get her in bed. Respect was an important part of any relationship. But had he read Sadie wrong? Had he reacted in a way that made her that uncomfortable?

It'd taken a few more beers once he'd gotten home to wash the bad taste of the night from his mouth and finally get some sleep.

Now fatigue made his movements slow and the pain in his head intensified with every step. With his gaze down, he made a beeline for his desk. Small talk was the last thing he wanted to participate in.

He reached his chair, but before he could sit his dad poked his head out of his office and yelled, "Wells, Pennel. In my office. Now."

Tommy groaned. Scratch that. Mindless chitchat wasn't the last thing he wanted. Sitting in a small office with Sadie was. He'd have to talk with her eventually, but he'd at least hoped for a giant cup of coffee first.

Hurrying across the congested space, he side stepped deputies, and entered the sheriff's office. He nodded a greeting at his dad, who'd taken a seat behind the messy desk, then plopped into one of two chairs in front of him.

Sadie entered. "Good morning, sir. Deputy Wells." Her voice was stiff, her words hard.

He didn't bother looking at her. She'd have the same pissy look on her face he'd witnessed for months. The one he'd finally erased when they were alone. "Morning."

"Shut the door before you sit, please."

Sadie did as asked then sank onto the seat beside him.

"Nice work last night. Both of you." Mike made sure to connect his cool, grey gaze with each of them before continuing. "Things could have ended a lot differently. I'm glad they didn't."

"Me too," Tommy mumbled.

"I've kept up with your reports the last few days. How does what happened last night with Mitch Parson affect your investigation?"

Tommy scratched the top of his head then rested his elbow on the arm of the chair. "We wanted to question Mitch today. He was on our list of suspects, given what we'd learned about Clara and Shawn's relationship."

"Do you still think Mitch is a suspect?" Mike hooked up one eyebrow.

"We weren't sure of his involvement since we didn't know if he was aware of the situation with his wife and Mr. Downs," Sadie said. "After last night, I think Deputy Wells and I can agree that Mitch learned of his wife's infidelity yesterday. If he'd known before, he would've taken his anger out on Clara a lot sooner."

Mike nodded. "I agree. He'll sit in county lockup until his hearing. You can question him as much as you want, but it might be a waste of time. I wouldn't put it past Mitch Parson to kill Shawn for sleeping with his wife, but it would have played out a lot differently."

"Agreed." Tommy wiped his hands on his pants. "Was there anything else?"

"I hate to micromanage, but I've got a lot of pressure coming down on me in regard to the Downs case. Where do things stand?"

Tommy shot a glance at Sadie. A lot went down between them last night, but discussing where their thoughts laid with the case wasn't one of them.

Sadie kept her back rigid, her focus forward. "We have an interview scheduled with Curtis McLane, the bar owner, soon. I also spoke with Shawn's roommate from college this morning. I'd like to find a girl he dated while in college, before he started dating Judge Downs. The roommate mentioned he spent most his time with her, and she might have more information. Besides that, the roommate didn't have much to say."

Tommy straightened. "You didn't tell me you spoke to the roommate."

She turned a stony glare on him. "I hadn't gotten a chance yet."

Heated words sat on the tip of his tongue, but he held them back. Arguing in front of his dad wouldn't be good for either of them.

Sadie faced forward again. "Deputy Wells and I also plan to look into Melissa Downs' habits and financials, if possible."

Mike frowned. "Why?"

Tommy bit back a groan, not wanting to get into the details with his dad right now. "Shawn had a large sum of money from a trust his mother established. With his death, the money goes to next of kin. It's standard to make sure there's nothing amiss with the person inheriting the money."

"Melissa Downs is well-to-do on her own merit. Digging around her personal life is bound to be messy and end in trouble the department can't afford."

Tommy clenched his jaw. "We also can't afford to gloss over any part of this investigation."

Mike sighed. "You're right. But tread lightly. Now go on. We've all got work to do."

Tommy rose and followed Sadie out the door.

"Curtis will be here in ten minutes. I have some things I need to put together before he arrives." She tossed the words over her shoulder as she marched toward her desk.

He stayed close on her heels. "What else did Shawn's old roommate say? Why didn't you let me know you'd talked to him?"

She kept moving, stopping once she reached her desk and shoving papers into a file folder. "He didn't tell me much. And I would have told you about it this morning when you got in. I didn't get a chance before getting called in to talk to the sheriff."

"You should have called me right away. I need to be up to speed on what's happened before we talk to our boss. I felt like an idiot finding this out while sitting in his office."

She shrugged, still rummaging around her desk. "That wasn't my intention."

"Dammit, would you look at me?" He dropped his voice to a whisper, but there was no way he could keep his anger from lashing out.

She stilled and lifted her gaze to his. "What do you want from me?"

He snorted. "Maybe an ounce of respect. First you assume I'm trying to get into your pants then you don't fill me in on an important aspect of *our* investigation."

Red slashes colored her face, and she pinched together her lips. She grabbed the file and held it to her chest. "I do respect you. And what happened last night...well, I don't want to get into that right now. Not when Curtis will be here any minute. We need to be focused on asking the right questions and nothing else."

Nodding, he worked his jaw back and forth. "You're right. About all of it. No need to discuss anything about last night. Not now or ever. It was a mistake."

Turning his back, he pretended he didn't see the flash of hurt that sparked in her eyes or feel the punch in his gut telling him the only mistake would be forgetting how amazing their kiss was.

Neither mattered. Not when he needed to convince himself he wasn't falling for the woman who'd thought the worst of him.

SADIE SAT NEXT to Tommy at the rectangular table set up in the conference room they used for interviews. The tension between them sat so heavy in the air it threatened to suffocate her. She yearned to clear up the nonsense and bring back the carefree banter they'd fallen into the last couple days, but she didn't know how.

Judging by the red bleeding through the whites of his eyes, he hadn't taken her reaction last night well. Hell, could she blame him? The guy held her while she cried and confessed her deepest secret, gave her the best kiss of her life, then she'd accused him of trying to get in her pants.

She clasped her hands on top of the table so she couldn't slap herself on the forehead. A million different scenarios paraded in her head while she'd tossed and turned in her bed the night before. If she wasn't so terrified of ruining her stupid reputation at the station, if she wasn't so scared to let down her walls, that kiss could have led to somewhere really freaking special.

A light knock on the door announced Curtis and tore her from her thoughts. His eyes were even more bloodshot than Tommy's. Grease weighed down his shoulder-length locks. He darted his gaze around the confining space before dropping it to his feet.

Sadie stood and offered him a smile. "Good morning, Curtis. Come on in and have a seat." She waited for him to move toward the vacant chair across from hers then closed the door before returning to her seat.

"Hey, Curtis. How are things?" Tommy's voice held a lot less hostility than it had earlier with her.

She cleared her throat and gathered her thoughts. Tommy's tone of voice or anger toward her didn't matter—at least not at the moment.

"I'm okay." Curtis lowered himself onto the hard, plastic chair. "I don't understand why you needed me to come here. We already talked. You could have just stopped by the bar again if you had more questions."

Tommy leaned his forearms against the table and gripped his hands around his biceps. "First why don't you tell me what you said to Mitch Parson yesterday?"

Curtis blinked, long and slow, as if closing and opening his eyes helped him process the question. "Mitch? Why do you want to know what we talked about?"

There was pale sheen to his skin that hadn't been there the

day before. Or maybe the harsh florescent lights emphasized his unnatural pallor. Either that, or the unexpected question had thrown him. "We just find it interesting that the information you gave Mitch didn't line up with what you told us. At least according to his statement." When Tommy had divulged how Mitch found out about Clara's affair, she'd been just as pissed as Tommy that they hadn't thought to make sure to talk to Curtis first to make sure he kept his mouth shut.

Curtis scratched thin whiskers poking through his chin. "I told you both the same thing. That Shawn had been talking to Clara."

"Are you sure that's all you said?" Tommy asked.

Curtis nodded. "Absolutely."

Tommy tilted his head to the side. "So finding out his wife had talked to Shawn was enough to push Mitch into beating her then threatening to shoot his kids?"

Horror filled Curtis's eyes. "What? Is everyone okay?"

"Yes," Sadie said. "No thanks to you."

"You don't understand. Mitch stormed into the bar. I had to tell him something. You don't know how he can get when he's all worked up."

Tommy picked up a pencil and tapped it against the table. "But you know. And it was better for you if Mitch took that anger out on his wife."

Curtis pressed his fingers against his eyebrow, his palm covering one eye. "No. You don't get it. That's not what happened."

Sadie sighed. She had no patience for a sniveling man who put himself first. "Honestly, it doesn't really matter now. What does matter is why you didn't tell us Shawn paid you every month, even though he was the one who worked for you. And funny how we haven't uncovered any income for him."

Curtis dropped his hand to the table with a *thunk*. "What are you talking about?"

"Don't play dumb," Tommy said. "You not telling us about this already looks bad. Don't make it worse by lying."

Sadie opened the file and pulled out copies of Shawn's bank statements. Red circles showed the consistent payments going from his account into Curtis'. "Care to explain?"

"Shit." Curtis ran a hand over the top of his head. "It's not what it looks like."

"What does it look like?' Tommy asked.

"Listen. Shawn and I always talked about opening a bar. He wanted to be a part of owning the place, even if no one knew. I tried to pay him, but he didn't want the money. Always said being needed was enough."

A pinch of sadness squeezed her chest. Everyone talked about how Shawn's life was a waste, that he'd gone on a downward spiral, but he really just wanted the same thing everyone did.

She tapped the paper in front of her. "That's an awful lot of money for him to hand over every month just to feel needed. And why didn't he want to be involved until after he inherited the entire trust? He worked at the bar before then. Did he have to contribute so much? Did you pay him before the trust became his?"

A line of sweat gathered along Curtis' forehead. "I don't know what you want from me. He came to me. He offered cash, and I took it. I'd put up with him hanging around the bar, pretending to work for years. I didn't see any issue in agreeing to take the money. I never asked for it. Never made a big deal of it."

"What happens now? Will the bar be in trouble since you won't be getting any more monthly payments from Shawn?" Tommy asked.

Curtis worked his jaw back and forth. "The bar will be fine."

Sadie wasn't so sure. Gathering the papers back in her file, she snapped it shut and studied Curtis' gaunt face as she slid out the picture she'd found in Shawn's bedroom. "What can you tell me about this photo?"

The side of Curtis' mouth slid up in a sad smile. "Damn. This was a lifetime ago." He grabbed the picture by the edges and lifted it, blocking his expression.

"When was it taken?" she asked.

He tossed the picture back on the table, his gaze still fixed on the smiling young faces staring up at them. "After Shawn and Mitch left for college. They both came home for a weekend, and we got together. Just like old times. It was never the same after that."

"Why's that?" Sadie pushed, sensing they were on the edge of something. Even if Curtis didn't realize what information he held.

"The next time Shawn came home was when his mom died."

Tommy straightened. "I thought Shawn came home every weekend to spend time with his dying mother before he dropped out. That he changed after she died?"

Curtis shook his head and tapped a finger against the glossy paper. "No. It was after this weekend. A few months before his mother passed on. Man, he loved that car. I wonder whatever happened to it?"

His statement tilted the reality Sadie had created in her mind. Now she just needed to find out what Shawn had done on that weekend so many years ago that changed the course of his life...and possibly brought an end to it years later.

16

Tommy cradled his head in his hands and kept his gaze on the door. Katherine told him she'd meet him at their favorite coffee shop fifteen minutes ago. Patience was never one of his strong suits—especially not when he was slightly hungover. The gut-punching scent of coffee made his stomach roll. The few cups he'd tossed back at the station still sat heavy in his stomach.

A bell rattled above the door. He lifted a hand as Katherine stepped inside and surveyed the crowded space.

She unwrapped her scarf as she approached the two-person table he'd secured in the corner. Grinning, she tossed a fast-food bag onto the table. "You sounded pretty rough on the phone. Thought the grease would be good for you."

Tommy opened the bag and inhaled the salty goodness inside. "You're a saint."

"Don't you forget it." She looped her coat and scarf over the back of the chair. "Give me a second. I want some coffee and need to kiss up to Lori since I brought in outside food. She'll probably make me buy a handful of cookies."

"You'd buy those anyway." He grabbed a French fry and shoved it in his mouth.

Katherine laughed and hurried toward the display window filled with pastries and deserts.

Tommy dipped his hand back in the bag and it brushed against a paper-wrapped burger. A deep groan rumbled in his throat. God love his sister. It didn't matter if he drank one or ten too many beers, a fast-food burger and fries were always the cure. He unwrapped the burger and took a bite. Grease all but exploded in his mouth.

Katherine slid onto the chair across from him with a cup of coffee in one hand and a pastry bag in the other. "Two cookies and one muffin. Not too bad."

Tommy chuckled.

"So, what happened last night?" Katherine took off the lid and blew on the hot liquid.

He shrugged. "You heard about what went down at Mitch Parson's?"

She took a sip then nodded. "You've seen tough stuff before. I don't remember it ever pushing you to drink. Hell, not much does."

He blew out a long breath. "You know me too well."

She grinned over the rim of her paper cup. "Sure do. So you might as well spill the beans."

"I wanted to talk over the case with you, not gossip about my personal life."

Scrunching her nose, she waved away his protest. "We have time for both. I want the dirt first."

He rolled his eyes and pushed away his burger. "Fine. Last night was rough. I followed Sadie home and walked her to her door. I just...I didn't want to go home alone." He shoved a hand through his hair. "I asked if I could come in."

Katherine widened her eyes. "You got drunk and stayed the night with Sadie?"

"No."

She furrowed brow. "Then what happened?"

"We talked, I kissed her, and I left." He wadded up what was left of the burger in its wrapper and threw it in the bag.

"And?" Katherine's steady regard could have burned a hole between his eyebrows.

He bit the inside of his cheeks to keep his anger from flaring. Hiding anything from Katherine would never happen. If he wanted to talk about the case, he might has well confess. "She accused me of trying to get her into bed." The words tasted like chalk in his mouth.

Katherine reared back her head. "Why would she say that? You didn't pressure her, did you?"

His jaw dropped. "Did you seriously ask me that?"

She shrugged. "Well, why else would she kick a handsome man out after kissing her if she didn't feel pressured?"

"Because she doesn't know how to let people in." The truth of his statement deflated some of his anger, leaving room for sadness to sweep over him. She'd been through a lot, and he couldn't blame her for hiding behind a tough exterior. But he'd thought they'd moved past that—had connected on a different level.

"Interesting." Katherine pushed together her lips.

"What's that supposed to mean?"

"You don't let people in either." She shrugged and took another sip of coffee.

He straightened. "Excuse me? I have tons of friends."

"You hide behind your charm and easy-going nature. But when's the last time you got this worked up over a woman? You may act like you go through life without things bothering you, or people crawling under your skin, but we both know that's not true. You only let people get so close."

Her words hit a little too close to home, and he shifted in his chair.

She softened her expression—lips turned down, eyes wrinkled at the corner, head tilted. "I don't want to upset you, but it's the truth. You're almost twenty-six years old and haven't dated anyone seriously since high school."

"Since Vanessa." He traced the scar on his cheek with his finger.

Katherine reached across the table and took his free hand. "I know how hard losing her was for you, especially right after Mom died. But you can't let that keep you from having something wonderful with someone else someday."

He squeezed his eyes shut for a beat, knowing what she said was true. But after living through the nightmare of losing not one, but two women he loved...the idea that it wouldn't happen again was hard to believe. Keeping women at arm's length was easier. "What does any of this have to do with what happened between me and Sadie last night?"

Katherine slid back her hand and grabbed a cookie from the pastry bag. "If Sadie has worked as hard as you to keep up her guard, you should understand why she'd say or do something ridiculous to stop someone from breaking through her walls."

Katherine's words rang true, but it didn't make it easier to hear or ease his injured pride at being thrown out of Sadie's house. "Can we talk about the case now? I want to pick your brain before I have to get back to the station."

Katherine smiled. "Fine. What's on your mind?"

"The lab called today. They gave me the make and model of the tires on the truck that rammed me onto the train tracks."

Katherine's smile disappeared. "Good. Any idea who it is?"

He shook his head. "The tire's pretty standard and used on a ton of vehicles. I want to look into autobody shops and track their sales. See if anyone local or on our radar purchased this brand or had them put onto a truck."

"Good idea. Is Owen helping you? It's gotta be driving him nuts to sit on the sidelines with this."

Tommy flicked a glance around the noisy room before speaking. "He actually hasn't overstepped at all. Has waited for me to approach him. I asked him to look into Melissa Downs. I don't have the skills he has, and Taylor is already busy."

Her frown deepened. "The judge? Why?"

Tommy rubbed a hand over his face. "She inherits all of Shawn's money. That's enough right there to shine a spotlight on her. Then there's their strange marriage. No one knows why they never divorced."

Leaning forward, Katherine rested her crossed arms on the table. "I always assumed Shawn was the one who refused to cooperate with the divorce. Maybe I was wrong, especially if large sums of money are involved."

"I talked to Patsy at the judge's office, and she mentioned everyone knew Melissa wasn't in love with Shawn. That she doesn't grieve his death. That doesn't jive with the behavior she displayed with Sadie at his trailer the night we told her Shawn was murdered. Something doesn't add up."

"I can poke around. Find out about their relationship. Shouldn't be too hard in this town."

A *ding* alerted him to a new text. He pulled out his phone and glanced at the screen.

"Everything okay?" Katherine asked.

"Yeah. Sadie's heading to the courthouse to look for files on Shawn."

"Do you need to go?"

He placed his device on the table. "No. I'll meet up with her when we're done." Digging through old, dusty files wasn't his idea of fun.

He'd let Sadie handle that while he finished talking with Katherine. Hopefully by then his subsiding headache would be gone and he'd have a better handle on how to move forward with Sadie. Regardless of how badly she'd hurt him the night before, he couldn't let it affect their working relationship.

They needed to focus on finding Shawn's killer. Then he could mull over Katherine's words and decided if he was ready to finally break down his own walls before he even tried to get through Sadie's.

A COLD DRIZZLE bordering between sleet and snow fell from the gray sky. Sadie wrapped a scarf around her neck, zipped up her jacket, and jumped out of her car. The station might be only a block away, but she didn't want to be outside in this mess any longer than necessary.

Hell, if she had a choice she'd pick up Amelia from the shelter and spend the day curled on the couch with hot chocolate and movies. She made a mental note to plan that for her next day off.

Bundling into the warm fleece, she lifted a gloved hand in greeting to Patsy. The judge's secretary was just stepping out of her car parked a few spaces down, but Sadie couldn't waste time getting sucked into a conversation.

And after witnessing Patsy and Tommy's relationship, she had no desire for the older woman to ask any questions about the partner she hoped to avoid for the rest of the day. He hadn't responded to her text, and she despised the disappointment that burrowed in her chest.

Pushing the unreturned text from her mind, she made a beeline for the front of the courthouse. She opened the door and a blast of warm air engulfed her, but it couldn't stop the shiver shaking her limbs. Peeling her wool hat from her head, she stuffed it in her pocket and hurried down the stairs that led to the basement. No one lingered in the wide hallway. She spied the room Owen had told her about and ducked inside.

The faint hum of the overhead lights filled the otherwise quiet room. Rows of metal filing cabinets occupied the space. Blasts of heat shot from overhead vents. Sadie shrugged out of her winter gear and draped it over one of the cabinets. She studied the front of the drawer. A small keyhole was in the middle of the drawer even though the cabinets were unlocked. A large cream-colored card labeled what was inside. As assumed, the first cabinet she'd come across contained files with citizens whose last names started with the letter A.

Following along the path of chin-high cabinets, she read each label and stopped when she reached the one that should house Shawn Downs' criminal record. She yanked open the drawer and flipped through, searching for the right one.

It wasn't there.

She started from the front and worked backward again, making sure none stuck together.

Still nothing.

Huffing out a breath of frustration, she scanned the rows of filing cabinets. If someone had misfiled Shawn's record, it would take days to search through this mess to find it.

Unless someone made sure the file didn't exist. Shawn's record not being available on the database at the station had been odd enough. Combined with it not being in its proper place in storage was downright suspicious. Nonetheless, she made her way up and down the congested aisles, searching for a logical place for the file to be.

She reached the back of the room, empty handed and full of questions. Sweat matted slips of hair from her ponytail to her temple. She grabbed her phone and checked the time. Forty-five minutes wasted.

She studied the bold lettering on the last cabinet. Cold cases. Facts and interviews tumbled around in her brain. A town the size of Water's Edge couldn't have too many open cases they kept tabs on. She slid open the door. The files in this drawer were labeled by year. Doing math quickly in her head, she flicked to the file from the year Shawn left for college. She pulled it, as well as the year after, from its space and closed the drawer.

Her fingers itched to search for anything that could be connected to Shawn, but she would wait until she got back to the station. She made her way to the front of the room. The sound of the door slamming shut reached her ears. She stopped, stilling every muscle in her body. Maybe someone walked by and closed it not realizing anyone was inside.

A familiar scent invaded her nostrils and stole her breath.

Smoke.

She quickened her pace. The thick, ashy smoke of something burning filled the room and stung her eyes. Where was it coming from? She raced to the door and turned the knob. The old brass handle didn't move. She shook it back in forth. "Come on. Open, dammit."

The smoke grew heavier. Flames licked up the side of the wall. She grabbed her scarf and tied it around her face, covering her mouth and nose. Panic threatened to pull her under. She couldn't let it. Lowering her shoulder, she banged against the door—over and over and over.

It didn't budge.

Tears filled her eyes. She grabbed her phone. No signal.

"Shit!" This couldn't be happening again.

The flames grew higher. She spun in a circle, searching for another way to escape. No windows, no other doors, no hope. Fear squeezed her heart. She couldn't go through this again. Not with a little girl waiting for her to come home. Her lungs burned.

She sunk to the floor to escape the increasing smoke and pounded her fist against the hard wood. "Help! Someone help me!"

17

Tommy brushed away the moisture clinging to his hair. The weather had gone from shitty to really shitty in the time he'd been in the coffee shop with Katherine. He'd needed the time with his sister—time to discuss the details spinning in his mind. No one could set him straight like Katherine. A new beat of determination lengthened his strides as he swept into the station and searched for Sadie.

She wasn't there.

No new messages or calls had come through from her. Could she still be at the courthouse? The possibility seemed slim. Grabbing what she needed from the basement should have taken little time. Unless she found something else that snagged her attention.

Taylor hovered by the coffee pot, stirring sugar into the mug that was a constant fixture on her desk.

He quickly erased the space between them. "Taylor, have you seen Sadie?"

Taylor stopped stirring and pulled her lips to the side. "Not in a while. She left and hasn't been back."

"Thanks." If Sadie was still in the file room, he needed to find out why. He grabbed his phone and pressed Call under her contact information.

No answer.

Dammit. The numbness hadn't left his fingers from the cold and now he'd have to go back outside. He couldn't just stay here and pretend her absence wasn't odd.

"Is everything all right?" Taylor asked, her brown eyes wide.

"Probably. I just need to find Sadie. See ya later."

Digging into his pockets, he found the gloves he hadn't been smart enough to put on earlier and covered his hands. Fierce wind blew against the door, making it more difficult than it should be to open. He hurried to the back lot and jumped into his car. He blasted the hot air and peeled out of the parking lot.

The courthouse loomed large, the ever-fattening flakes dimming the appearance of the bright red bricks. Tommy parked the car and climbed out. He jogged up the steps to the main doors, stepped inside, then hurried toward the staircase that led to the basement.

He descended the stairs at a clipped pace, and a familiar scent invaded his nostrils. Like a bonfire, but more pungent. He quickened his stride, sounds of his footsteps echoing off the ceiling. A faint banging mingled with the beat of his steps. Fear invaded his chest. Something wasn't right.

He ran. The hallway was thick with smoke. The banging grew louder, more frantic. The smell of something burning became stronger. He flew around a corner and plumes of smoke billowed from under a closed door. A chair was wedge under the knob, ensuring that anyone inside wouldn't make it out.

"Help me! Please!" The voice was dim, wispy.

His blood pressure spiked. *Sadie.*

"Fire!" He threw the chair out of the way and yanked open

the door. A wall of heat barreled against him. Sadie, crouched low to the floor and pressed against the barrier, fell forward. Soot marred her face, hiding the freckles he loved so damn much. He scooped her into his arms.

"Wait." The word croaked from her mouth. "The files. Grab them. Should be by the door."

He spotted the files through the thickening smoke. He grabbed them and ran toward the stairs. He pulled out his phone to call for help, but he didn't have a signal in the basement. Sadie was light as a feather in his arms. Her fingers curled around his jacket, and she buried her face against him. Her chest rose and fell in a slow, steady rhythm. Her breathes came out in ragged gulps. Smoke inhalation was just as dangerous as the fire.

Once he reached the first floor, he checked his phone again. Finally, a signal. He called dispatch. "There's a fire in the basement of the courthouse. Get the fire department and ambulance here now. Pull security footage and talk to everyone who was inside. Someone trapped Deputy Pennel inside with the fire. Someone tried to kill her."

Billows of smoke rose from the basement. He disconnected and headed toward the front door. A red fire alarm was secured to the wall. He yanked down the handle and bells of warning blasted into the air. Water rained down from the sprinklers inserted into the ceiling.

A middle-aged man with thick round glasses poked his head out from a nearby office. "What's going on?"

"There's a fire in basement. Get out now. Help's on the way." Not wasting another breath on a further explanation, he rushed back out the door. The man's panicked yell hit him in the back of the head, but he kept moving.

He burst outside. Sadie shook and huddled closer to his chest. Sirens signaled help was near. He took the narrow steps two at a time. People poured out of the building behind him. Panicked questions tossed around with the wind.

Firetrucks and police cars peeled into the parking lot. He jogged to one of the two ambulances.

An EMT, Eric, jumped down from the cab. "What do we got?"

"Deputy Pennel was trapped in the room that caught on fire. Lots of smoke. Don't know how long she was in there." He carried her to the double doors in the back of the ambulance.

Eric opened the doors wide.

Tommy climbed into the back and lowered Sadie onto the gurney. Her death grip kept him close. He curled his palm against her dirty cheek. "You're okay. I've got you."

Tears ran down her face, leaving trails through the ash built up on her cheeks. "Locked in. Again." Tremors overtook her body. Her lips shook, the color turning a scary shade of blue.

"She needs oxygen." Eric crammed into the crowded space and grabbed a tank and mask. He fit the clear mask over Sadie's mouth. "Take nice, slow breaths. Let me check your vitals before we head out."

Sadie nodded. Her teeth chattered. Shock was setting in. The smoke and the fire combined with the fear of being locked in a literal inferno was bad enough. But add the trauma of the past and it was more than anyone could take.

Eric listened to her heart and checked her pulse. "Okay. Let's get you to the hospital. Keep the mask around your mouth. Fill those lungs with nice, clean oxygen, okay?" He jumped out of the cab and closed the doors.

Tommy set the files she'd insisted he grab on the floor and shrugged out of his jacket. He tucked the coat around her slim frame. "Everything's okay."

She shook her head. "No. Why? Why did it happen again? The screaming. I could hear them screaming in there with me. But I was alone. Why am I always alone?" Her eyes slid closed.

He didn't have to ask who she meant. Her nightmare had become her reality, blurring the past and present into one moment of hell. The raspy quality of her voice and the anguish of her words tore at his heart. "Hey. Look at me."

She lifted her eyelids and locked her gaze on him.

"Do you trust me?"

She nodded.

"I'm here, and I'm going to take care of you. Will you let me do that?"

"Yes."

Pressure built in his chest, threatening to crumble his composure. The motion of the ambulance taking off had him swaying. "Good. We'll be at hospital soon."

"Okay." Her eyelids closed again, and she let her hand drop from his shirt.

People continued to pour out of the mouth of the courthouse, fear and panic evident on their faces.

Had one of them seen something? Known some sick sonofabitch had started a fire and locked a woman in a room to die? Anger pulsed through his body with every breath. Someone had tried to kill Sadie. And when he found out who, Tommy would make sure the asshole paid.

THE HURRIED FALL of footsteps shuffling outside the curtained-in space ruffled in Sadie's ears. The distinct smell of a hospital—a not-so-subtle fusion of disinfectant and sickness—battled with the overpowering scent of smoke absorbed in her uniform.

She hated hospitals and all the memories attached to them. Work brought her to the emergency room more than she'd like, but usually it was to speak with witnesses or accompany a criminal who needed attended. Not sitting scared and wheezing on a hard mattress, waiting for a doctor to clear her.

Tommy leaned forward in the chair he'd placed right next to the bed. An unnatural paleness washed out his normally vibrant features, making the scar on the side of his face stand out. He bounced his knee up and down, a sign he was just as uncomfortable sitting in the emergency room as she was. "How are you feeling?"

She cleared the crud from her throat. "Better."

"I should have been there with you. I'm so sorry." Worry shone from his hazel eyes. He clenched and unclenched his fists as they sat on his knees.

"You have nothing to apologize for." Craving the comfort he'd given her the previous night, she gathered all her courage and rested a hand on his.

His gaze shot up to meet hers.

"You saved my life. No way I could have made it out of there on my own."

Opening his hand, he flipped it palm up and wrapped his warm fingers around hers. "As soon as we get out of here, we'll talk to the Fire Marshal. Someone started that fire. Did you hear anything? See anyone? Even before you got to the basement. Maybe you noticed someone lurking as you went inside."

She shook her head. Her hair swept in front of her face, and she cringed. The loose strands were saturated in smoke. She'd need to wash it soon or the smell would plague her. "I got to the courthouse and parked, waved at Patsy, then hurried inside. I was in the file room for about forty-five minutes. The door slammed closed, which was odd. The smell of smoke hit me first, then the fire. I tried to get out, but the door was stuck."

Her heart rate kicked up at the memory. She closed her eyes, determined not to break down again. She'd let herself fall apart once, now she had to keep it together and tell Tommy exactly what happened. If she couldn't go over the details, they'd never figure out who'd started the fire.

The mattress dipped and warmth wrapped around her shoulders.

Smiling, she opened her eyes and leaned against Tommy. For once, she didn't care who walked in—who saw her giving in to the primal need for human connection—she relaxed against his side and evened her breathing. Calmed the beat of her heart. "I thought I was going to die." Her whispered words competed with the beeping monitors.

Tommy rested his forehead on her temple. "I'd never let that happen."

The curtain flew open. Sadie straightened, but she kept her hand secured in Tommy's.

Concern and fear shone through Katherine's tight expression as she marched to the bed and threw her arms around Sadie. "Thank God you're all right."

Warmth and acceptance washed over Sadie like a spring rain—welcomed and desperately needed. "What are you doing here?"

Katherine pulled away and hoisted a tote bag off her shoulder. "I brought you clothes. Tommy called when you got here. He figured you wouldn't want to wear clothes that smelled like they'd been dried over a campfire. You're a little smaller than me, but these should work for now."

Tears of gratitude formed in her eyes. "Thank you."

"It's the least I can do." Katherine set the bag on the vacant chair. "You doing okay?"

"Yeah. Just want to get out of here."

Katherine smiled. "I totally understand."

Loud footsteps pounded toward them. Sadie raised her brows and glanced at Tommy, who shrugged. The curtain pulled back again, and the Sheriff barged in.

Tommy tightened his grip on her hand. A fleeting thought

of pulling away tempted her, but she stayed put. Even after the sheriff dropped his gaze to their joined hands, over to Katherine, then back to Sadie's face. "Deputy Pennel. Are you okay?"

"I'm fine, Sheriff."

He huffed out an annoyed breath. "Please, call me Mike. I spoke to the fire department. The damage was contained to the basement, but the scene at the courthouse is a mess."

"Has anyone checked the surveillance cameras?" Tommy asked.

Mike yanked his hat off his head. "The cameras show someone go to the basement, throw something in the room, and slam the door close. The suspect wore a large black hoodie and covered his or her face."

"You guys must be getting close to finding the killer," Katherine said. "First someone went after Tommy. Now Sadie. They want to stop you."

"From what?" Sadie threw up her free hand and another cough tore through her. "I didn't even find any records for Shawn. Someone made sure there was no trace of any of his wrongdoings."

"What about the files you made me grab?" Tommy asked.

"Cold cases from the year Shawn graduated high school as well as the following year. I thought maybe something would stand out we could tie to Shawn. Something that could help make sense of this mess."

Katherine sank down into the chair. "That would be the year before I graduated."

Tommy released his grip on her hand and rubbed a palm over his face. "Shit."

Sadie turned wide eyes on him. "What is it?"

Mike cleared his throat, gaining her attention. "That's the year their mother was killed."

A boulder dropped in the pit of her stomach. "I...I'm sorry. I didn't know. I just grabbed them."

"No, it was good thinking. Something could be in those files we hadn't considered." Tommy squeezed her knee.

"He's right," Mike said. "Smart move. But it appears as though you two have already made someone very nervous. Have you talked to anyone who could have gotten spooked?"

Sadie gasped. "Curtis McLane."

Katherine tented her brows. "You think he's capable of not only murdering Shawn, but coming after two sheriff's deputies?"

Sadie shrugged. "We talked to him again this morning. His finances aren't lining up. We let him know we were looking into discrepancies in his statements. It just doesn't add up that he's taken money from Shawn all these years."

"True," Katherine said. "But why take out the person who's giving you money? Why put your business at risk?"

A dull ache built in Sadie's forehead. Between the smoke inhalation and the mounting questions, a migraine was sure to attack soon.

Tommy stood and cool air rushed in to take his place, leaving her yearning for him to stay. "I've wondered the same thing," he said. "We need to speak to him again. Now. We'll squeeze out all the information he's hiding. One way or another."

18

Tommy entered Sadie's house and rubbed the back of his neck. He tossed the files he'd brought in from the car on the side table pressed against the wall. The physical connection she initiated at the hospital led him to believe she'd gotten past their misunderstanding last night, but he couldn't leave the status of whatever was going on between them to assumptions.

She cast a glance over her shoulder as she kicked off her boots. "I won't take long. I just didn't want to show up to interview a suspect in your sister's yoga pants and baggy sweatshirt. Not to mention my hair reeks."

"No problem. I can make some calls while you get cleaned up." In the shower. Naked. Wet. He swallowed hard and tried to erase that tempting image.

She straightened and frowned. "What calls?"

"Local autobody shops. I want to check to see if anyone sold any tires recently that match the treads of the ones left near the train tracks."

Her shoulders deflated. "Good idea. We really need a break in this case."

He absently crossed one arm over his ribs. The pain had subsided but the memory remained. "A lot has happened the last couple days." Fear of her reaction held his tongue for a beat. He swallowed, keeping his gaze trained on her face. "Like what happened between us."

She swiped her tongue over her lips. "About last night—"

He held up a hand, the need to get his words out before whatever excuse she presented weighed heavy on his chest. "I'm sorry if I crossed a line. If I misread your feelings. I should have just listened. That wasn't the time or place to kiss you."

She closed the distance between them, her eyes wide and unreadable. "I'm sorry. You've been so kind, so nice to me. You've brought me and Amelia around your family, introduced me to friends I could have if I'd just give a little bit of effort, and were there for me when I desperately needed it. That kiss..." Sadie pressed her fingertips to her mouth.

"You don't have to say anything else. It's fine. I can take a hint. Friends are important and I will always be around for that. Even when the case is solved, and we've moved on to different things." He shrugged and offered her a small smile even though an unexpected knife twisted in his heart. He wanted to know so much more about her, wanted to be around her daughter and get more drawings of rainbows to hang on his fridge.

Dropping her hand and her gaze, she bit into her bottom lip.

The silence spurred him on. "I can be there for you whether it's listening to you talk on your living room couch or holding your hand in the hospital. You aren't alone. Never again. I understand that's all it is, and I won't put you in a shitty situation again. Scout's honor." Tommy held up his hand in the Boy Scout salute he'd learned as a kid.

"That's not what I want." She spoke the words so softly, he swore he didn't hear her correctly.

All the moisture evaporated from his mouth. She pinned him to the spot with her eyes, full of hope and nerves. "I'm really doubting my ability to read you right now, so I need you to spell it out for me."

She grinned. "Don't all men?"

He hooked up the corner of his mouth. "Don't really want to hear about what you've had to do for other men."

She laughed then sucked in a deep breath, all amusement fleeing from her face. "I panicked last night. Telling you what happened in Iraq was something I never intended to do—never intended to tell anyone. But in that moment, a little bit of the weight I've carried so long was lifted."

"I'm glad. You shouldn't have to shoulder that burden alone."

"Then you kissed me, and I swear to God the world tilted. That's never happened before, and it scared the hell out of me. I mean, how is it possible that in a few days you've gone from this cocky, carefree playboy to a genuine, kind man who rocked my world with a simple kiss?"

"Rocked your world, huh?" he asked, purposefully overlooking the less than flattering opinion she'd carried around of him.

She rolled her eyes. "I'm being serious. I never want to make you feel bad. Or make you think you've made me uncomfortable."

"So I didn't push you too far?"

"You pushed me, but in a good way. You made me see how much I've held back—from you and everybody in this town. I've kept people from getting close to me. I don't want to do that anymore. It stops now." Stretching onto her tip toes, she pressed her lips to his.

As much as he longed to hold her against him and take this kiss to a more comfortable spot than the hallway, now wasn't the time. Now was the time for sweet promises and showing Sadie she could depend on him. That he'd be there for her and her daughter no matter what.

Breaking the contact, he smiled down at her. "I'm glad we got this cleared up, but you really stink."

She threw back her head and laughed. "How on earth did I ever think you were a womanizer with smooth words like that?"

"I've been a lot of things in my life, but a womanizer has never been one of them. Go on and get cleaned up. I'll be out here waiting."

She pressed a quick peck to his cheek. "Make yourself comfortable. Food's in the kitchen if you're hungry. I won't be long."

He watched her hurry down the hall and disappear into the bathroom before he fell into the soft sofa with his phone in hand. A lightness settled over him, despite the situation he'd stumbled into. A situation that had led danger to him and Sadie.

But for one small moment, his world was perfectly centered. A hope for a future with someone he could really care about dangled before him. He just needed to make sure he didn't mess it up....and that they solved this case with both of them making it out alive.

VANITY HAD Sadie adding a touch of concealer to hide the bags growing under her eyes and swiping gloss over her lips. Her hair, however, was useless. Not that it mattered. She had a job to do, and that job required her hair to be pulled back. Not long and loose where it'd just get in her way. But the look of appreciation shining from Tommy's eyes when she emerged made her forget any insecurities regarding her unruly hair and freckles.

"You ready?" She forced out the words. Going back into the freezing cold to track down a killer who'd just locked her into a burning room was about as tempting as sticking her head in the oven. Especially when she and Tommy seemed to have reached an understanding. Staying in her nice warm house, losing herself in his arms, sounded so much better.

Shooing Mittens from his lap, Tommy stood. "Sure thing. You sure you're up for talking with Curtis again? No one would think twice if you took the rest of the day off."

As tempting as the thought was, she couldn't. "I need to be there. Need to see his eyes, watch his body language when we confront him. Something's not right. I wasn't convinced he was our guy, but now I'm not so sure."

"Let me know if you need a break, okay?" He dipped his chin, leveling her with his stare.

"Fine." She grabbed the keys Tommy had left in her white dish by the door. "You want to drive?"

"Sure."

She tossed him the keys and grabbed a coat from the closet. "Let's go."

The sun hung low in the sky as late afternoon crept in. The gray clouds had lifted, letting shafts of golden rays highlight the sparkling crystals casing the ground. Snow covered her walkway, erasing their footprints from earlier. She trudged a path to the car and settled into the passenger seat. Her lungs burned and the migraine she'd predicted beat behind her eye.

Tommy started the engine, cranked up the heat, and pulled onto the country road that led straight into town.

"Did you get any useful information from your phone calls? Maybe get some answers on that damn key we found?" Resting her head against the back of the seat, she turned her neck to take in the view of his strong profile.

He snorted. "That key is a pain in my ass, but I did get some answers about the tires. I got ahold of the only shop in town, as well as one town over. Both have tons of records of sales for that specific brand of tire. The managers were helpful, and agreed to dig a little deeper and find out if any tires were placed on a full-sized truck in the last twelve months."

"Hopefully they can provide some more names to look into. With Mitch in jail, Curtis is our best suspect."

Tommy cast her a quick glance before swinging his gaze back to the road. "Maybe we'll crack through whatever bullshit he keeps throwing at us and lock this thing down today."

Hope beat back the fear still clinging to her psyche. She held onto it as Tommy slowed to the snail-pace speed limit and parked on the street in front of the bar.

"Shouldn't be much of a crowd," Tommy said as he shut off the car and slid the key from the ignition.

"At this point, I don't care if we have to interrogate the bastard on a stage in front of the whole damn town. I just want this over with." She stepped onto the sidewalk and waited for Tommy to round the hood before heading for the entrance to Town Tavern.

Tommy opened the door for her to enter then followed. A few customers sat at the bar, huddled over their beers or snacking on peanuts. Highlights from last night's big game dominated the big screen that hung above the wide selection of spirits.

"I don't see Curtis." Sadie scanned the room. Patrons occupied a couple of tables, but the place was mostly deserted. But even though people didn't fill the tables, empty glasses and plates littered the unused seating. "This place is a mess. Is that normal?"

"Not at all."

A pretty, young waitress hustled through the swinging door from the kitchen with a plate in each hand. Her face was screwed in a knot, irritation coming off her in waves.

Tommy raised his arm. "Ashley. We need to speak with you for a minute."

"One second." She didn't even stop to spare them a glance as she slid the plates in front of two older men at the bar then refilled their beers from the tap.

"Let's take a seat." Tommy dipped his head toward the closest table.

"Good idea." Her whole body ached as if she'd run a marathon. Another side effect of being thrust into a living nightmare and barely making it out alive. *Stop it. Put what happened out of your mind. Focus.*

Straightening her shoulders, she perched on the edge of a wooden chair and studied the bustling server. "Does she usually work alone? The lunch shift ended a little while ago, but it looks like no one's been here to help."

"Curtis is usually always here. Unless he's in the kitchen, which I doubt, looks like Ashley dealt with the earlier crowd by herself."

The skin on the back of her neck puckered. If Curtis hadn't been here most of the day, it would leave him without an alibi when someone locked her in the file room.

Ashley rushed over. Her cheeks were flushed, and she used the back of her hand to brush red bangs from her eyes. "You want to order? Sorry. Today's been a bit nuts."

"Where's Curtis? Isn't he working the bar?" Tommy asked.

She clenched her jaw. "Nope. Boss hasn't been around today."

A rush of adrenaline invaded Sadie's veins. "When's the last time you saw him?"

Ashley shrugged. "This morning. Came in to work the breakfast shift, saw him leave, then took a break before lunch. He wasn't here when I got back."

"Did you ask the cook?" Sadie wondered.

"He heard Curtis clomping upstairs to his apartment before

he stepped out for a minute. He went up and knocked on the door, but no one answered. Assumed Curtis left and hasn't been back, the ass." Ashley covered her mouth. "Sorry. It's been a rough afternoon."

"Totally understandable." Sadie forced a smile then focused on Tommy. "Maybe we should go knock. Maybe he didn't hear or was under the weather."

"Good idea. Is it okay if we head upstairs for a second?"

"I don't see why not. You can go through the office so you don't have to use the outside entrance."

"Thanks, Ashley," Tommy said and stood.

"No problem." She turned and rushed back toward the kitchen.

Sadie followed Tommy to the back of the bar to Curtis' office. Papers were scattered all over the card table-turned-desk and a computer hummed in the corner. The desire to linger and casually flit through the mess slowed her gait, but she couldn't do anything stupid. She didn't have a warrant to search the office—at least not yet.

An opening on the far side of the cramped space led to a stairwell much like the one that led to Tommy's apartment. Most downtown establishments were probably built the same. Business on the bottom, apartment on top.

She stayed close to Tommy as they climbed the stairs. A loud pop sounded, and dread settled in her stomach. "That was a gunshot." She guided her gun from its holster.

Tommy pounded his fist against the door. "Curtis! Are you in there? It's Deputies Wells and Pennel."

No sounds came from the other side of the door.

"Ready?" he asked.

"Yes." She tightened her grip, holding the gun at the ready.

Tommy grabbed the knob and turned. "It's unlocked."

Her heart galloped, her palms moist.

Tommy burst open the door. "Shit."

She entered the apartment behind Tommy, the scent of blood and death engulfing her. Horror made her want to stumble back outside, but she held her ground.

Sitting at a table was Curtis with his head down, blood pooling from a gunshot wound on his temple.

19

Tommy took a second to check his gag reflex at the door. The iron-like smell of blood assaulted his nostrils. But it was the brain matter splattered against the wall that almost had him heaving his burger from earlier.

Sadie sidestepped him and moved further into the apartment. “Gunshot wound to the head. Gun’s on the ground under his hand, which is dangling at his side. Looks self-inflicted.”

Sucking in a deep breath through his mouth, Tommy rounded the table. Thick blood covered the wood and dripped onto the floor. “Dammit. How long has he been sitting up here?”

“Do you think we freaked him out?” Her voice wobbled a bit before she cleared her throat.

“Maybe. What’s that under him?” He slowly approached Curtis. A piece of paper, white except for the blood smears, poked out from under him. Tommy pulled a pair of rubber gloves from his pocket and carefully slid out the paper. “All it says is ‘Sorry’.”

Sadie hurried to join him, peering over his arm at the paper.

"Apology for killing Shawn? Maybe the guilt along with knowing we set our sights on him pushed him over the edge."

"It's typed out. You think he sat down, typed out one word, printed it out, then shot himself?"

She shrugged. "Maybe."

"I don't know. Doesn't feel right. Not for a guy like Curtis."

"We need to call dispatch."

He grabbed his phone and made the call. "Deputy Pennel and I are at Curtis McLane's apartment. Appears to be dead. Self-inflicted gunshot wound to the right side of the head." Realization dawned on him. Closing his eyes, he brought a memory of Curtis pulling the tabs on the draft beer to his mind —his left side facing the door, his left hand pulling the lever. "Send the crime scene unit. Now." He disconnected and shoved his phone back in his pocket.

"What's going on?"

"He's left-handed. He always pulls the lever on the tap with his left hand. I'd swear it." He darted his gaze around the room. There had to be another way to prove which hand Curtis preferred. "If I'm right, chances are slim he'd use his right hand to aim a gun at his own head."

"That would mean he didn't kill himself. He was murdered." Sadie pulled out her weapon. "We need to clear the apartment. I don't think someone would hang around, but we can't risk it."

Tommy nodded, his throat tightening. He grabbed the gun he'd put back after spotting the body. "The setup here is just like my place. Kitchen, living room, short hall with a bathroom on one side and bedroom on the other."

"Kitchen's obviously clear," Sadie said, scanning the narrow room.

Tommy nodded and headed into the adjacent living room. The open concept made checking the room unnecessary, but he didn't want to take any risks. He nudged aside a heap of blankets, opened the closet by the front door, then crept toward the back of the apartment.

Next, he checked the bathroom. He stepped inside while Sadie waited in the hall. The room was so small, there was no space for the both of them. The dark blue shower curtain was pushed to one side, giving him a clear view of the inside of the shower. Nothing stood out, nothing shouted a killer had been here.

"One more room to go." Sadie pivoted toward the bedroom. The door was ajar, and she bumped it open with the toe of her boot.

The unmade bed was pushed against the wall. A television sat on a corner stand, a dresser took up most of the far wall, and a desk finished off the space. He moved in behind her. She checked under the bed while he opened the closet. Clothes jammed together on one side of the closet, a wooden filing cabinet on the other side. "No one's here."

"Didn't the server mention something about another entrance? One accessible from outside?"

"It's the door at the end of the hallway." He pivoted out of the bedroom. Wind carried in from a small slit around the edge of the door. "It's not closed all the way." He flung it open and stepped out onto the fire escape. He scanned the area below. Footprints marred the thick snow—one set coming and one set going. "We need deputies canvassing the area. Those prints could be from Curtis, but if they're someone else's, we have to know if anyone saw who they belong to."

He tipped his head toward the interior of the apartment. "The place needs searched. I'd classify this as a suspicious death."

"Agreed."

Wanting to give himself a few more minutes before viewing Curtis's dead body again, he moved back into the bedroom and stopped in front of the filing cabinet in the closest. "Do you want to do the honors, or shall I?"

She wrinkled her nose. "I've had enough of filing cabinets to last a lifetime. You go for it. I'll make the call to get deputies to search the area while I look through the rest of the room."

He gripped her bicep, giving what he hoped was a reassuring squeeze. "You doing all right?"

Sadie sighed. "Fine. Let's just get this over with." She grabbed her phone and rattled off the information to the dispatcher, then silence fell upon them.

He turned back toward the storage and pulled open the top drawer. "He's got a ton of papers stuffed in here. Nothing's in an actual file. It's just jammed inside."

"Business or personal?" Sadie asked from the other side of the bed. "His office was a disaster downstairs. Maybe he stores some of the paperwork from the bar up here."

He grabbed a fistful of loose papers and flipped through. Some receipts, some notes on food distribution. A computer printout caught his attention. Names lined the side of the page with notes on each. "Holy shit."

"What is it?" Sadie crossed the room to stand behind him.

"He's got names of people from the town written down with snippets of information on each of them."

Her body pressed against his back as she tried to catch a glimpse of what was in his hands. "What kind of information?"

"Who they've dated, where they work, people they have beef with." He flipped over to the next page. "Same here."

"You said the bar was a good place to gather gossip. Looks like you weren't the only one who thought so."

Disgust swirled in his gut. "I wanted to learn about the citizens of the town so I could help. Not keep tabs on them to use for whatever the hell this is." He shook the paper, anger pounding through his veins.

Sadie gripped his shoulder. "What if he used it for blackmail?"

He turned, facing her. "What do you mean?"

"Think about it. He was getting money from Shawn on a monthly basis. What if Shawn didn't want to be a part of the bar, like Curtis claimed. What if Curtis had dirt on Shawn and used it for extortion?"

"Have to be one hell of a secret to get that kind of cash from Shawn."

Sadie shrugged. "If the secret was big enough to kill over, it would be big enough to cash in on. Maybe Shawn didn't want to pay anymore. Curtis wouldn't have liked that."

Thoughts pounded against his skull. What Sadie laid out made sense, but it didn't feel right.

A knock sounded from the front of the apartment. "Wells. Pennel. You here?"

"Is that the sheriff? What's he doing here?" Sadie asked, confusion etched on her brow.

"I don't know anything anymore. Let's see what he wants." Tommy led the way back down the hall to the kitchen.

His dad examined Curtis's body from a few feet away. "Sonofabitch."

"Our thoughts exactly," Tommy said. "What brings you here?"

Mike aimed a stony-eyed glower in their direction. "I just got a call. Clara Parson bailed out her husband this morning. Mitch Parson is on the loose. No one knows where he is."

Tommy swore. The news was like a blow to the gut. Just when he thought his day couldn't get any worse, something else happened to turn his day to shit. He glanced down at Sadie, whose face had turned a sickly white. "Well, if Curtis's didn't shoot himself, looks like we've got another suspect."

~

Sadie paced back and forth across her living room. A bone-weary sadness weighed down her entire body, but she couldn't stop moving. The day had dragged on for an eternity with still no answers and another dead body. The only bright spot in the last couple of days was Clara getting away from her asshole husband.

Thank God Marie had driven Amelia home earlier. Tommy had entertained her while she'd prepared dinner then put her over-tired daughter to bed. Guilt lingered after she'd given her a goodnight kiss and closed the door behind her. Amelia was having a magical school break filled with baking cookies and watching movies, but she was doing it without her. Once the case was solved, she'd make it up to Amelia tenfold.

Tommy stood in the archway that separated the kitchen from the living room, his feet wide and arms crossed. "I can't believe she bailed him out of jail. What the hell was she thinking?"

"Abused women stay with their abusers all the time. It's a vicious cycle. One that's almost impossible to understand from the outside." Sighing, she ran a hand through her hair. Her entire childhood was centered around a woman who didn't know how to stop that cycle.

"I hate that she feels obligated to him," Tommy said.

"Good thing it's too late to go speak with her." She faced Tommy and pressed her hands to her stomach. "I have so many emotions swirling inside me. I don't think I could have kept a cool head."

"You need sleep. It's been a long day and you've been through the ringer."

"My nerve endings are literally buzzing, like I just downed ten espressos. My eyelids are so heavy, but I don't know if I could even sleep if I tried." Frustrated tears threatened to fill her eyes. She blinked them back.

Tommy extended a hand. "Come here."

She fell against him. "My mind is spinning."

He smoothed a palm up and down her back. "I know. It's nothing we need to think about now. Put it out of your mind."

She huffed out a humorless laugh. "Easier said than done. Do you think Mitch could be behind this? We agreed he'd have acted differently if he'd known about Clara."

The pecs beneath her cheek rose and fell. "He might have played us. Knew his history would point to lashing out at his wife as soon as he learned of the affair. He could have gone after Shawn then bided his time before punishing Clara."

"That's so vile. If we find out that is what happened, he's a lot smarter than we gave him credit for."

"When we figure out what happened, we'll make sure whoever is responsible for all this shit goes down. But right now, you need to quiet your mind and sleep."

She hugged him tight. "You're right."

"Are you okay by yourself, or do you want me to crash on the couch?"

She smiled against him. She was an army-trained veteran. If there was one thing she didn't need, it was a man around her house to protect her. Plus, the first time she had Tommy stay the night, she wanted him in her bed and not the couch. "No, I'll be fine."

He skimmed his knuckles up and down her arms. "I should get going then. Let you rest."

Part of her wanted to take back her earlier words and ask him to stay, but that's not how she wanted to start this relationship. She squeezed him tight then took a step back. "I'll see you in the morning."

Tommy gently brushed his lips to hers. "Can't wait."

She watched him shrug into his jacket and walk out the door, sending her a wave before closing it behind him. Giddiness lifted her spirits as she locked up, turned off the lights, and headed for her bedroom. Shedding her uniform, she found her warmest pajamas and slipped under the down comforter on her queen-sized bed.

Her mind raced a mile a minute. She flipped on the lamp beside the bed and the files she'd brought home caught her attention. Putting the events of the past few days out of her mind wasn't a possibility, but maybe immersing herself in a new angle could at least help make sense of things. Grabbing the top file, she skimmed the highlights of page after page.

Her gaze landed on Tina Wells' name. *Tommy's mom.* Her breath caught in her throat. She devoured every detail on the sheet. Tears misted in her eyes. Tina had been taking an evening stroll when a car jumped onto the sidewalk, hit and killed her, then took off. The only witness was a teenager from across the square—the only relative information provided that the taillights fleeing the scene were from a car as opposed to a large truck or SUV.

The ache in her soul intensified. She understood how crushing it was to lose someone she loved, but she knew exactly what happened to Amelia's father. The not knowing had to keep the wound open, festering.

She tossed the files on the nightstand and clicked off the lamp. Exhaustion filled her eyes with grains of sand—her brain finally overloaded to the point of explosion. Sleep was her only option at this point, and her body was finally ready to succumb. Lowering her eyelids, her breathing slowed and she fell into the blessed darkness of slumber.

SADIE JERKED AWAKE ON A GASP. Goosebumps erupted on her arms despite the flannel pajamas and thick down blanket. Intuition tingled the back of her neck, as if eyes were on her. She stilled her body, listening for any unfamiliar sounds. Not even her crazy cat jumping around the house vibrated the ancient floorboards.

Moving her arm slowly from under the covers, she secured the sidearm she kept in a locked box and tucked inside the drawer of her nightstand. She slid off the safety and crept onto the balls of her bare feet. She locked down the nerves threatening to tremble and put on her game face. If someone was stupid enough to break into her home, they'd pay a hefty price.

After turning on her lamp, she lowered herself to a crouch and lifted the bed skirt. Nothing but a storage container with her summer clothes and a few dust bunnies. She rounded the end of the bed and swung open the closet door. Clothes hung on the hangers, everything in place. She poked through the articles of clothing then turned to check the rest of the house.

With her gun trained in front of her, she swept into the hall and padded toward Amelia's bedroom. Holding her breath, she cracked the door and a whoosh of relief crashed against her to see her daughter sleeping peacefully in her bed. A quick search of the small room showed Sadie nothing had been disturbed—no one waited inside.

Giving Amelia once last glance, she hurried to the living room. Mittens lay curled on the couch, undisturbed. Maybe she was being paranoid. Mittens would be long-gone if he'd heard someone breaking in. She checked the front door and a bit of tension released when she found it locked.

She headed into the kitchen and flipped on the light. She checked every nook and every corner. Nothing was out of place. But that tingling sensation still lingered on the back of her neck, muscles knotted in her stomach.

Needing to make sure the whole house was safe, she checked the bathroom and guest room. She dropped her arm to her side. The closets were clear, and doors secure. She had lost her mind.

Mittens padded out to meet her in the hall. She scooped him up and carried him back to her room. Maybe a little company was what she needed to settle her down and get back to sleep. Tucking her gun back in its place, she huddled under the covers while the cat curled against her side. She pillowed her hands under her cheek and her gaze landed on the nightstand.

The files were gone. Her heart seized. Panic hitched her breath.

She grabbed her phone with a shaking hand and called Tommy.

"Hello? Are you okay?" His voice was thick with sleep.

"Someone was in my house. I need you. Now."

20

Tommy's heart was in his throat by the time he flew up Sadie's driveway and slammed his car in park. The full moon beat a bright path down her unshoveled walkway to the front porch. He leapt up the steps and the door swung open before he could get to the doorbell. A long gray robe wrapped around Sadie's small frame. Her hair rained around her face in wild waves.

She hugged her middle, her eyes wide. "I knew someone was here. I could feel it. The files are gone. They were right by my bed, and now they aren't. I checked everywhere for them." Her jumbled words came out at a rapid speed.

"Nothing else was taken but the files?" He tried to keep a steady head and get the facts. She'd been frantic on the phone, the information she'd given garbled.

"Everything's in place. I triple checked."

"How did someone get in? Are all the windows locked?"

She squeezed the bridge of her nose. "All but one. I cracked open the bathroom window earlier when I showered. The house is old, and the room doesn't have a vent. The space fills up with so much steam when I shower that I always open the window to let it out. With everything going on, I must have forgotten to lock it."

"Did you check outside?"

She nodded. "Once I knew the house was secure, I walked the perimeter. Tracks in the snow led to the road on the side of the house. Plows had already been through, so no tire tracks."

"No way anyone saw anything way out here. Especially at this time of the night. We can have someone come check for fingerprints. We might get lucky."

"Done. I'm trained and had the equipment here. I'll send it to the lab in the morning."

Astonishment overrode the fear that had taken residence in his gut since she'd called and told him about an intruder in her home. This woman could do anything she put her mind to. Whoever broke in better count their blessings she hadn't caught them. No telling the amount of damage she would have inflicted.

"You secured the house, walked the perimeter, checked all entry points, and dusted for fingerprints." He held up his hand and ticked each action off the pads of his fingers. "What did you need me for?"

She dropped her arms to her sides and sniffed back the emotion taking over her face. "They could have hurt Amelia. Could have gotten to my daughter and I'd have never known until it was too late."

He was such an idiot. He crossed the distance between them in three long strides and grabbed her tight. She was so damn capable of taking care of herself and her daughter, it slipped his mind for an instant that she shouldn't have to. "I'm sorry. What I should have said was you are amazing and strong and so courageous."

"Someone was in my house. While I slept. Anything could have happened. I wouldn't have been able to defend myself—

wouldn't have been able to defend Amelia. Not when I was sleeping."

"That didn't happen. They took what they came for and left." He held her close, wanting to take away whatever fear remained. "You're safe. Amelia's safe."

"I just keep thinking, how long was this person here? Where did they hide? It's such an invasion of privacy...of my personal space."

"Do you and Amelia want to stay at my place tonight?" He cringed while waiting for her response. In no way did he want her to think he was using this situation to his advantage. But if she didn't feel safe in her home, he'd gladly give up his bed for the night. Hell, he'd give up his bed and hunker down on the couch for as long as she needed to feel secure again.

She pulled away and wiped the moisture beading on her lashes. "I just don't want to be alone. I'm sorry I dragged you out so late. You don't need to drive back across town. Why don't you stay here?"

He stilled, weighing his words so he didn't say the wrong thing. "You sure? Earlier you wanted me to leave." As much as he wanted to stay, he didn't want her to regret anything. Even if it was only him crashing on her couch.

She wrinkled her nose. "Earlier my home hadn't been violated."

He smiled. "I'd be happy to stay. I don't like the idea of you being alone until this is over. Do you have an extra pillow and blanket I can use?"

"You can't share my blanket?" She bit into her lower lip. Vulnerability shone from her wide eyes.

Excitement stirred in his gut. He mentally stomped it down. "You want me to sleep with you in the same bed?"

"Would you mind?"

He belted out a laugh and pulled her close again. He

pressed his lips to the top of her head. "You are unlike any woman I've ever met."

She wrapped her arms around him. "Is that a good thing?"

"A great thing."

She released her grip and took his hand, leading him to her room.

He stood in the doorway, taking in the no-frills room that matched the rest of her house. The sky-blue comforter lay rumpled on the bed. One frame with a picture of Sadie and Amelia sat on her nightstand. Nothing scattered on the floor or cluttered up the furniture.

Sadie removed her robe and hung it on a hook attached to the back of her door.

How in the hell could she look so damn sexy covered in baggy flannel?

She flipped off the light and sat on the edge of the bed, eyes trained on him.

His pulse raced. Hesitation over what to do next kept him frozen to the spot. He'd never spent the night with a woman he was falling this hard for. Not even Vanessa. Their love had been pure and still innocent when she was ripped away. The heat overtaking his body demanded he sweep across the room, gather her in his arms, and show her just how much he wanted to be with her.

But another part of him told him to take things slow. She'd been through hell today. Then there was the issue of how to sleep. At home, he stripped down to all his glory. But he couldn't just take off his clothes and hop into bed with her.

"I can practically see the wheels in your head spinning," Sadie said with a wicked grin.

He chuckled and squeezed the back of his neck. "I don't want to make you uncomfortable—don't want to take things too far too fast."

"I just invited you into my bed. Stop overthinking."

Stepping further into the room, he shrugged out of his jacket and laid it on a chair in the corner. He peeled off his shirt, tossing it to join the coat. He rested his fingers on the button of his jeans. No way he'd be able to sleep with the stiff fabric covering his legs, but he could be crossing a line to slide in next to her with nothing on but boxers.

Sadie giggled. "Do you need me to turn away?"

"Shut up," he said on a laugh. He unbuttoned the pants, glided them down his legs, and approached the bed. "You better get your fine ass under the covers before I do something that keeps us up both awake for a very long time."

She stared up at him and circled her mouth with her tongue.

A low growl rumbled from deep in his throat. "Sadie." He spoke her name as a warning.

"I don't want to go to sleep right now," she said, her voice low.

His chest tightened, his heart lodged in his throat. She was so damn beautiful, and he didn't want to mess anything up. He wanted to do things right this time. "Are you sure?"

She nodded and rose to her knees. Hooking an arm around his neck, she pulled him close.

Her body molded to his, her skin so hot and tempting he almost melted. He tucked a strand of her hair behind her ear then lifted her chin so her eyes met his. He studied every line of her face, the long curve of her neck, and committed this moment to memory.

Then he kissed her.

21

Tommy's chest rose and fell in rapid succession as he tried to regulate his breathing. Sweat coated his hairline. Sadie lay tucked against his side with his arm draped over her bare shoulder. He caressed her silky skin. Desire stirred in the pit of his stomach despite spending the last couple hours in her bed, moving in rhythm with her and fulfilling a deep need in his soul he never knew he had.

Sadie roamed the tip of her stubby nail through the mat of hair on his chest. Her warm breath skimmed his skin.

He pressed his lips into the tangle of chestnut waves matted against the side of her face. "You're magnificent."

She giggled and turned onto her side, propping her chin on her hand. "We're not going to get any sleep tonight."

He cringed. "I don't even want to look at the clock. But no matter how tired I am in the morning, this was totally worth it."

She grinned down at him. "You better say that." Her smile fell, and she traced her slender finger along the jagged scar on his cheekbone.

He stilled, waiting for the questions he knew would come. The scar was a constant reminder of his painful past. But for the first time, he wanted to tell a woman about everything that had haunted him for so many years. If he wanted a real relationship with Sadie, he had to lay all his cards on the table.

Moonlight spilled in through the parted curtains and cast a glow on her creamy skin. Her freckles stood out, and he touched them with his index finger. "I love your freckles. Have I told you that?"

Shaking her head, she remained silent with her gaze locked on him.

Words lodged in his throat. She was waiting for him to open up—wanting him to be the one to make the choice to confide in her. The need to confess, to tell her everything, electrified his nerve endings. But it was so damn hard.

"You don't have to tell me. It's okay." The smoothness of her voice calmed him.

He shivered out a breath. "I want to. I just don't talk about it very often."

"Take your time. I'm not going anywhere."

He shifted to stare at the ceiling. His pulse raced as memories flooded him. "I've only ever had one serious girlfriend. Her name was Vanessa. We went to school together and started dating freshman year. Right before my mom died." Recollections tightened his esophagus, making the last words come out in a higher pitch than normal.

The motion of her hand on his face stopped.

"She was my best friend. Helped me through the loss of my mom the way no one else could." Pressure built in his chest, and he squeezed the bridge of nose to keep his emotions from boiling over. He'd talked about this a hundred times, but it never got easier. Whoever said time healed all wounds was full of shit.

"It must have been nice to have someone like her around to help." Sadie hiked up her knee and nestled it on top of his thigh.

The feel of her body spurred him on, comforted him. "After Mom died, Vanessa and I were always together. She made me laugh, showed me joy, taught me that even amidst pain and heartache there could be happiness." He let his eyelids drift closed. He could see Vanessa's long black hair swirling around slim shoulders. Dazzling blue eyes sparked with mischief and a wide smile that always knocked him on his ass.

Sadie settled back onto her back and rested her head on his shoulder. "What happened?"

The image of Vanessa vanished, and a picture of twisted metal and busted glass swept in to take her place. His eyes flew open, unable to keep the scene in his head. "We went to the movies one night. She had just gotten her license. Her parents didn't want her driving in the dark, but I convinced them it'd be fine. The theater was only a couple miles from her house, and I'd be with her. What could go wrong?"

Her body tightened and she gripped his hand, as if bracing for the impact of his admission.

He clung to her like a lifeline. His throat was raw, his eyes burned, and his gut twisted into a million knots. But he needed to get it out—all of it. "On the way home, the roads were dark and a little slippery. Vanessa pulled up to a four-way stop. I saw the headlights coming toward us and told her to wait. She laughed, saying the truck would stop. Then it slammed into us." Tears sprang to his eyes, but he didn't bother to dash them away.

A beat of silence hung over them before Sadie whispered, "It wasn't your fault."

He shoved his free hand through his hair and gripped the finger-length strands trapped against the mattress. "My head knows that. But the way her parents looked at me. Like if I hadn't talked them into letting us go to the movies, Vanessa would still be here...that look has haunted me every day. Because even though it wasn't my fault a drunk driver ran through a stop sign and hit us, I was the reason we were there. I was the reason we were in the car on the road that night." The pressure in his chest threatened to explode, and his sinus cavity throbbed. Tears flowed freely down his cheeks, but he couldn't care less.

"I'm sorry you lost her, and I'm sorry you were hurt. Is that what the scars are from? The car accident?"

He nodded. "I was banged up pretty bad. Nothing I couldn't bounce back from. All the bones healed, the gashes long gone. But the scar stayed and reminds me every day of the part I played in losing the first girl I've ever loved. After losing her...losing my mom...it was too hard to put my heart out there again. I couldn't handle anyone else being ripped away."

She squeezed his hand, and her breath tickled his collarbone. "I could lay here and tell you that feeling guilty about something you couldn't control is useless. But that'd make me a hypocrite. I get it. I understand carrying a burden you shouldn't bear on your shoulders because knowing it's there gives you this weird, sick sense of peace. Like if you feel the guilt every day, you're keeping them alive."

Propping herself back on her elbow she glanced down at him with the most tender look he'd ever seen. She released her grip on his hand and traced the pad of her thumb over the scar that told a story so much deeper than the ugly line on his face. "But we've been doing it wrong. Carrying around shame and guilt over the loss of these people doesn't do anything but bring us down. Getting lost in the sadness of your past makes it impossible to keep the positive memories of a girl you loved so much alive. Just like the blame I heap on myself stops me from living the life I truly want."

He closed his hand over hers and brought it to his lips. Her words rang so damn true, but he didn't know if he could let go of the way he'd lived—the way he viewed his past—for so long.

He wanted to, God he wanted to more than anything. "Thank you for that. But now I think it's time we both get some sleep."

Leaning forward she pressed her lips to his then snuggled against him. "Thank you for telling me."

He lay there, listening to the sound of her breathing slow until he was sure she'd finally fallen asleep. Her words played on repeat in his mind. If she could learn to let go of the guilt she'd wrapped around her like a shield, then he could try to do the same regarding the part he'd played in Vanessa's death. Especially if he had Sadie by his side.

TOMMY BURIED his hands deep in the pockets of his coat. Every inch of him wanted to be all over Sadie, but morning had come and he'd had to leave before Amelia woke and Sadie shuttled Amelia back to the shelter for another day of 'helping' Mrs. Collins. He wanted to be as much a part of the little girl's life as he did Sadie's but catching him in her home first thing in the morning wasn't the best way to ease her into having him around.

Besides, they had work to do. No matter how much he yearned to reach for Sadie, standing on Clara's concrete stoop was not the place or time for physical contact. Even if he wanted to risk it, Sadie would slap him.

He smiled, despite the seriousness of what they were about to walk into. Last night was incredible. Energy fueled him and he was filled with excitement despite the lack of sleep. But he had to keep all those new feelings tucked away until he could get Sadie alone again. Not only had the sex been amazing, but he'd woken this morning feeling lighter than he had in years. Bearing his soul to her had been tough as hell, but it had lifted something he hadn't even known he'd needed to let go of.

He stole a glance at her as she pressed the doorbell.

Snowflakes settled onto her sleek ponytail, her mouth set in a firm line. He'd give anything to kiss her stupid and bring back the wicked grin that had played on her lips most of the night before.

"I hate this house," Sadie said. "I hate what it represents."

"Hopefully we won't have to come back after today."

The door opened a crack, and Clara's red-rimmed eyes peered out at them. "Mitch isn't here." Gone was the frantic woman they'd seen a few nights ago, terrified of losing her children. Back was the timid, abused wife with meek words and nowhere to turn.

"Do you know where he is?" Tommy doubted she'd tell them even if she did know.

Clara shook her head. The bruise circling her eye had turned a nasty shade of purple with tinges of green and yellow mingling along the outside. "No, but he isn't coming back."

"Does he have any friends or family he would stay with? Anyone who'd let him crash on their couch?" Tommy couldn't think of anyone Mitch hung around with. Most people couldn't stand his explosive temper.

She lifted a shoulder. "He doesn't have many friends. His parents still live in town. They don't speak to each other much, but if he needed a place to stay, they'd probably let him."

He didn't want to alarm Clara even more by letting her know Mitch's parents had already been questioned and had no idea where their son was.

"Do you know where he was yesterday after he got out of jail? It's very important we find him. We need to make sure he won't hurt anyone else." Sadie kept her voice calm and steady.

"He left. He's not coming back." Tears filled Clara's eyes. "I don't know what I'm going to do. How can I raise these kids on my own? I can't do anything on my own."

Fear radiated from her and made his pulse race. He hadn't

known Clara when she was younger, but he'd guess all her self-doubt came from years spent under Mitch's thumb.

"You can do anything you want, Clara. I promise," Sadie said. "There are people who can help. The card I gave you the other night has all the information you need to contact the women who run Safe Haven Women's Shelter in Pine Valley. Call them. Please. But I have to know. How are you so certain Mitch won't be coming back?"

Clara blew out a long, defeated breath. "As soon as he got out of jail, he came here and packed a bag. Said he was done with me and didn't want anything to do with the kids. Then he took off. I haven't heard a word from him since."

"What time was that?" Tommy asked, trying to create a timeline in his mind.

Clara nibbled her lips and darted around her gaze. "Umm, I'm not sure. I secured the bail money first thing in the morning. I had to pick him up about an hour or so after that. So the last time I saw him was probably around ten. In the morning. It couldn't have been much later than that."

Her jumbled rambling was hard to follow, but all he needed to hear was the time. And if she was right, that meant Mitch was unaccounted for during the fire at the courthouse and when Curtis was shot. "Did he take his gun with him?"

Clara crinkled her forehead. "I have no idea. I didn't look."

"It's important we know that information," Sadie said. "Your husband may be out on bail, but that doesn't mean he's free to do as he wishes. And if he's armed, that's something we should be aware of."

"Oh. Okay." She held the door open wider. "You can step inside and wait while I check."

Tommy stepped in behind Sadie and let the door close. The television blared from the living room. Davey, the toddler, sat with wide eyes on the screen. If he didn't know any better, he'd never guess this little boy had been terrified of his own father hurting him a few nights ago. But most scars ran deeper than the surface, and there was no telling when they'd appear and haunt this poor kid. Clara might not agree right now, but Mitch leaving was the best thing for her and her children.

The boy glanced over, and fear filled his eyes.

Tommy kept his features relaxed, even though his insides curdled.

Sadie crouched onto her heels in front of the child. "Hi, Davey. Do you remember me?"

He nodded.

"What are you watching? I love cartoons. Can I watch with you while we wait for your mom?"

He nodded again, but this time a whisper of a smile lifted his mouth.

Sadie plopped onto the floor next to him. Davey inched his little hand closer to Sadie's until he nestled it inside her palm.

Tommy's heart flooded with all kinds of emotions he'd never experienced before. He loved being around his niece and nephew, and he got a huge kick out of Amelia. But seeing Sadie slide in and comfort a kid who'd been through hell made things turn to mush inside him he didn't even know could be mushy.

Clara hurried back into the room, her arms hugged tightly around her middle. "His gun's not in the safe."

Sadie rose to her full height. "Do you know the model of the gun? Is it registered?"

The weapon Mitch had on his lap while Tommy stood defenseless in front of him flashed in his mind. Revolver. The same gun they'd found in the room with Curtis.

"I'm sorry. I know I'm not much help." Clara dropped her gaze to the top of Davey's head. "I'm worthless."

Sadie pivoted, blocking Clara's view of her son. "Look at me, Clara." She waited for the other woman to meet her gaze before she continued. "You're stronger than you know. You have two children who depend on you, and you will get through this. Do you understand me?"

Uncertainty danced in Clara's eyes.

Sadie rested a reassuring hand on Clara's arm. "Will you make that call?"

"Yes."

"Good. There's an entire community ready to help you. Just give them the chance."

Clara brushed away tears dotting the corners of her eyes with a trembling hand and nodded. "Thank you."

Tommy couldn't tear his gaze off Sadie—not that he wanted to. Her stern reassurance to a woman she barely knew made his heart double in size. She was a warrior. Gentle yet strong. And if he had any doubt before this moment, any trace of uncertainty vanished. He was falling head over heels for Sadie Pennel.

22

Sadie sat at her desk with her chin propped on the heels of her hands. Her list of things to do lay in front of her, but she couldn't stay focused on any of the tasks demanding her attention. Not when Clara Parson's defeated eyes refused to stop haunting her. She'd do everything in her power to make sure Clara led a full, healthy life without her bastard husband by her side.

"What's with the face?"

The smooth, deep voice sent a shiver down her spine, and she glanced up to the handsome smirk and deep dimples that now made her toes curl. "What's wrong with my face?" She smiled, despite the turmoil churning in her gut.

Tommy took his now-usual spot on the side of her desk—perched on the corner with his long legs sprawled out before him. "You look like someone just ran over your puppy."

She wrinkled her nose. "I don't have a puppy, but thanks for the visual."

He huffed out a laugh. "Sorry."

She dropped her arms, crossing them on the cool wood of the desk. "I hated seeing Clara so freaked out about her future.

I barely know the woman, but I can't push her out of my mind. I've met so many women like her over the years. No matter how much I try to give back, I know there will always be more women like her out there."

Tommy picked up the piece of paper from her desk. "The infamous to-do list. I see you've added some things. Some of which have to do with Clara."

Her eyes latched on to his large hands gripping the sides of the sheet. Flashbacks of what he could do with those hands slammed against her. Tingles of anticipation burst like fireworks.

"Sadie?"

She blinked herself back to the present. "I want to touch base with Laura. I'm not convinced Clara will reach out for help. Not when she's spent years hiding in that nightmare of a house. She'll need support, for her and the kids. Laura's been in that situation. She may know the best way to reach Clara."

He nodded, keeping his eyes on the lined paper. "I agree. Who is Jess Sproles?"

"Shawn's college girlfriend. The one he dated before he started seeing Melissa. I sent her a message on Facebook—couldn't locate a number yet. Hopefully she responds so I don't have to keep wasting time trying to find it."

"Look into Curtis' confiscated computer, search for connections between Shawn, Curtis, and Mitch, speak with Judge Downs." Tommy read from her list then glanced up. "What do you want to speak with her about?"

"Have you ever been inside her home? I thought maybe Shawn could have left some things in the house that could be of interest. Maybe she'd let us snoop around."

The clomp of boots came toward them, and Sadie was surprised to spot Taylor. She brushed snow from her shoulders and offered a wide smile. "Hey guys. What's new?"

"Sadie wonders if Judge Downs will let us check out her

house." The lines on Tommy's raised forehead nearly touched his hairline.

"Good luck," Taylor said with a small snort. "I can't help you with that, but I did find something interesting before I grabbed some lunch."

Tommy sat Sadie's list back on the desk and stood straight. "What's that?"

"A storage unit in Shawn's name. He's been paying for one monthly for years." She fished a slip of paper from her back pocket and handed it to Tommy.

Tommy frowned. "Why would he rent a storage unit two towns over?"

"Good question," Taylor said. "Especially since I checked other storage units in town and the one Shawn's been using is more expensive."

"A storage unit would be locked, right?" Sadie asked, wheels spinning.

Tommy tilted his head to the side, brow furrowed. "Most likely."

She grinned. "Where'd you put that key?"

THIRTY MINUTES LATER, sunlight reflected off the snow-covered fields, nearly blinding Sadie on her drive to Litchman. The storage units sat on the outside of town, cutting down on the drive time. Her pulse hummed as she neared the city limits. This could be the break they needed.

As long as the damn key worked. If not, it'd take a little bit of time to wade through the red tape to get into the unit.

Tommy sat beside her with his phone in his hand. He waded through digital files he'd been sent by Owen and updates on Curtis' case. At this point, most of the precinct was trying to figure out what had happened to the bar owner and the part he played in Shawn's death.

One thing was certain, Curtis hadn't killed himself. Water's Edge either had two killers on the loose, or someone willing to silence anyone who got in the way. Sadie's money was on the latter.

The entrance to the storage facility loomed a few miles ahead and to the left. "These places creep me out."

Lifting his head, Tommy stared out the window. "You mean you don't like spending time in the middle of nowhere with a bunch of little structures that could be hiding anything?"

A nervous laugh bubbled in her throat. "You nailed it."

She drove past the sign announcing her arrival to Litchman and came to a halt at a stop sign. Tommy hooked a thumb to the left, and she turned toward the cluster of buildings and into the entrance of the storage facility, then navigated down the rows of squat units.

Slowing the cruiser to a crawl, she studied the units. Bright orange roofs adorned shabby, off-white rectangular structures. Little black numbers marked small garage doors, giving an indication of the size of the spaces.

"There's the one we want." He pointed ahead, a couple units down in the wide, gravel aisle.

She came to a stop in front of the number Taylor provided. She drew in a deep breath to clear her head then cast Tommy a let's-do-this look. "Ready?"

He nodded.

Turning off the engine, she exited the car and pocketed her keys.

Tommy rounded the hood of the cruiser and joined her in front of the miniature garage door. He inserted the key then lifted the door until the rusted barrier disappeared from view. "Bingo. Finally found the missing lock to this damn key."

The sunlight was enough to chase away the shadows inside. A large structure under a cream-colored cloth dominated the majority of the space. Otherwise, the room was empty.

"A car?" Her voice echoed off the concrete floor and cinder block walls. Stale air settled inside her nostrils and bits of dust floated in the sunbeams.

"Judging by the layer of dust covering the cloth, no one has touched the car in years." Tommy crouched, lifting the end of the material draped over the car. "Help me get this thing off."

Stepping to his side, she grabbed a fistful of the thick cloth. Working together, they rolled it up until they could toss it to the other side of the hood. The momentum carried the material over the other side where it landed with a heavy *thud*.

Her jaw went slack and her blood pumped furiously through her veins, threatening to make her heart explode. The red sports car matched the one in the picture she'd found of Shawn and his buddies.

TOMMY GAPED, stunned into silence. Of all the things he'd expected to find in the storage unit, Shawn Downs' old car wasn't one of them.

"This is the same vehicle from the picture I found at Shawn's trailer. When I showed it to Curtis, he mentioned how much Shawn loved this thing and wondered what happened to it." The confusion in Sadie's voice matched what was building in his head.

He rounded the driver's side and whistled. "What happened indeed. Check out the front fender and windshield. Completely busted up."

She moved slowly to his side and studied the smashed headlight and dented metal. "Why store a busted-up car you love? Why not fix it up?"

Tommy chewed the inside of his mouth as he thought on the question and considered the fractured glass on the windshield. "If it were someone else, I'd say maybe they didn't have the money. But that's obviously not an issue."

Straightening, Sadie made her way around the rest of the vehicle. "Don't see any other scratches or dents. Only damage is the front."

He scratched his jaw, unable to tear his gaze from the damage. "So impact came head-on. Then what? He hid the car and forgot about it? Why the hassle? Why pay money every month to keep it here?"

"Because they didn't want anyone to know what they hit."

Her words made his stomach muscles clench.

"Someone took the plates off." She snorted. "What idiot thinks taking the plates off will make it hard to identify the owner? We can just check the VIN number. Not to mention the fact that we already identified the renter of the unit."

"Let's see if anything's inside." Wanting to be as careful as possible, he secured his hands inside a pair of gloves before opening the driver's side door.

The interior was immaculate. He leaned in and opened the center console and glove box, finding both compartments empty. No better luck under the seats on in any cracks or crevices.

Sadie slammed the trunk closed as he backed out of the car. "Nothing in the trunk."

"Dammit." He grabbed his phone and opened the camera, making sure to snap pictures of the VIN number and the destruction. "Might as well verify this is Shawn's car to cover all our bases."

"We know when Shawn rented the unit, and we know when Shawn dropped out of college and returned home. How can we figure out what happened between those times?" Closing her eyes, Sadie pressed her fingers against the middle of her forehead.

His gaze traveled back to the cracked windshield and his

blood turned cold. "We look at hospital records in the area. Search destruction of property in the county around those times."

Her eyes snapped open. "What?"

"Whoever was driving this car—probably Shawn—hit something or ran into something big. First, we figure out what caused this damage, then we figure out why they wanted to make sure no one found out."

Sadie drew in a quivering breath. "I don't like where this is heading."

"Neither do I. But hopefully it will tell us everything we need to know about Shawn, which then leads to his killer."

She nodded. "Let's get out of here."

"Help me put the cover on first."

They secured the heavy cloth then stepped out of the small space back into the sunlight. Tommy grabbed the handle on the garage door and yanked it down, making sure to lock the unit back up.

A gunshot rang out, vibrating the metal door.

Tommy dropped into a crouch, Sadie right beside him. With his back pressed against the aluminum garage door, he grabbed his gun while his heart thumped an erratic rhythm. He glanced to his side but couldn't see a damn thing on the other side of the cruiser. "We need to get in the car."

Staying low, Sadie took one step then another. She pressed her back against the driver's side of the car and reached for the handle.

Bang!

The bullet collided with the front of the vehicle.

The buzzing adrenaline in his veins stalled. Putting himself in danger was part of his and Sadie's job, but he'd never faced the opposite end of an unknown gunman with the woman he was falling for by his side.

Sadie covered her head with her hands and froze, her wide eyes fixed on him.

He held his breath, wishing he could cover her body with his to keep her from harm. But she was smart and capable. Not to mention any sudden movement on his part could put them both at risk. He kept his gun trained in front of him, his gaze darting from side to side.

She hooked her fingers under the handle and pulled, opening the door. She jumped inside, staying so low he couldn't see her once she was in.

A sigh of relief escaped his lips. She was safe. Now he needed to get his own ass inside.

He glanced in the direction of the shot. A shadow shifted on the end of the building to his left. He lifted his gun and pulled the trigger. The shadow skittered away. Tommy leapt toward the open door.

Sadie thrust her keys at him. "Take the keys."

He grabbed them and shoved the key into the ignition while he scanned in all directions.

"I think your shot scared whoever it was off." Sadie sank against the seat, her gun at the ready.

An engine revved to life. A truck shot out from behind the building at the end of the lane and toward the gated entrance.

Tommy pressed his foot against the gas pedal. Gravel flew up and pinged the side of the door.

The truck drew closer. This was their chance to catch the sonofabitch. Adrenaline *whooshed* in his ears.

Sadie took aim and shot out her open window, the sound splitting his ear drums. "I don't think I hit anything."

After a moment of silence, a sudden pop had him reflexively hunching his shoulders. The front window exploded. Bits and pieces of glass nicked his exposed skin. He kept his gaze locked forward as he took a sharp turn toward the entrance, trying to see through the shot-out windshield. "Shit. Can you get off another shot? Aim for his tire."

Nothing but the sound of racing wheels on a bumpy country road answered him.

He flicked his glance toward Sadie. His heart lodged in his throat, and he fought the urge to stop the car.

Sadie sat slumped against the seatback, eyes closed. Blood trickled from the side of her head.

23

Mumbled curses penetrated the thick fog of unconsciousness that had turned Sadie's world to black. Weights held her eyelids in place. Movement jostled her body, causing spikes of pain to spear her head. She moaned, but the dry cotton of her mouth trapped the sound. Air rushed at her as if she was caught in a wind tunnel.

Willing her eyes open, she winced as sharp beams of light attacked her retinas. She lowered her eyes to narrowed slits. Pain slammed like a sledgehammer against the side of her head. Stinging bites throbbed around her face.

Tommy sat beside her. His hands gripped the steering wheel. Cold air whipped through the open window beside her...and in front of her. Glass sprinkled the dashboard.

She bent at the waist, curling forward with her head in her hands. Warm liquid slid over her fingers. She reared back and nausea pitched in her stomach. Blood covered her trembling hand. Images of bloody soldiers and dying civilians invaded her thoughts, making her limbs quake, quickly replaced by the smiling face of her daughter.

No, she couldn't be hurt. Couldn't *not* go home to her daughter tonight.

She swallowed the bile that rose to her throat with each bump in the road. She kept her focus on the worried lines indented in Tommy's handsome face. "Tommy?" The sound of her hoarse voice was unfamiliar to her own ears.

Tommy whipped his head to the side, his eyes wide and mouth pressed in a tight line. Raw fear dilated his pupils. "Don't move. You've been shot. The bullet grazed the side of your head. We're almost to the hospital." Emotion made his words come out thick.

"The truck.... where's the person who shot at us?" She tried to crane her neck to glance behind them, but her head screamed in protest.

"I called dispatch." He returned his focus to the road as they drove through Litchman. "A patrolman was close by. When I took off for town, the truck went in the opposite direction. No idea if they'll catch the bastard or not."

Tommy's gentle touch caressed her arm. "Lean back. We're almost there. Just stay still. Everything's going to be fine." His touch might be soothing, but he couldn't hide the worry that clipped his words.

She collapsed against the seat. The siren on top of the cruiser wailed as they raced through the quiet streets. Head wounds bled heavily, regardless of how bad the blow. The sharp pricks of pain on her face told her the blown-out window had pelted her pretty bad. But it was the throbbing agony on the side of her head that demanded attention.

Unwrapping the scarf from around her neck, she pressed the material to the oozing gash at the side of her head. She needed to be smart, not succumb to the panic clawing at her psyche, which meant stopping as much of the bleeding as possible.

Tommy moved his fingers along her arm until he peeled

into the emergency room entrance of the hospital and screeched to a halt. He shut off the engine and jumped out of the car, racing around to her side.

Two doctors dressed in green scrubs raced out the emergency room doors with a gurney between them.

Tommy opened her door. "She was grazed by a bullet on the left side of her head. Lost consciousness for a few minutes. The marks on her face are from the glass." He tossed his statements over his shoulder, keeping his gaze trained on her.

She reached for his hand, attempting to climb from the car.

One of the doctors rushed forward. She had a warm smile and steady, familiar green eyes. "Stay still, Sadie. It's Jenna—Dr. Simon. If you have a bullet wound, I want to know the extent of the damage before moving you."

She swallowed hard and locked her gaze with Tommy's. His take-charge attitude calmed her, and the hint of terror and emotion clinging to him made her heart dance despite the constant pain in her head.

He stayed within view as the doctor carefully lowered her hand and peeled away the scarf. Blood trickled down the side of her face. "You're lucky. Looks like the bullet barely grazed you. You'll need some stitches and a CAT scan. I'd also like to tend the cuts from the glass." Dr. Simon glanced over her shoulder. "On both of you."

The pressure squeezing her chest loosened. The agony in her head was still intense, but she would be all right.

"Let's get you inside and cleaned up."

Dr. Simon stood and motioned the other doctor forward. He approached, rolling the gurney close to the car. "Do you need help, Deputy?"

"I can do it." She gritted out the words, needing to prove she was capable.

Tommy wedged himself between her and the doctors. "I got her." Leaning forward, he cradled one arm around the small of her back then hooked her elbow around his neck and swept her into his arms.

The movement made dizziness swim in her head. She closed her eyes on a long beat to regain her equilibrium, squeezing her arms tight around Tommy's neck.

Tommy lifted her onto the gurney. "Lay down and relax."

Refusing to leave her side, he clung to her hand as he helped wheel her through the emergency waiting area and into a curtained-off room. The thin, blue curtains might have blocked off the rest of the area but did nothing to shut out the chaos on the other side. The smell of bleach coated the air.

"I'll get started on you, Sadie. And my colleague here, Dr. Perkins, will take Deputy Wells right next door." Dr. Simon softened her voice, but her order came through loud and clear.

"I can wait," Tommy said.

Sadie smiled up at him. Spots of blood dotted his face from the broken glass. She winced. He had to be hurting. "I'm all right. Go. The sooner we're both taken care of, the sooner we can leave."

Dr. Simon analyzed the sterilized tools lined up on a tray beside the bed. "We'll talk about your evening plans when I'm done."

Tommy lingered beside her, certainty wavering.

She pushed back the pain, not wanting to give him more reasons to demand he stay at her side. "I'm fine. Go."

"All right. I'm right next door if you need me."

Sadie watched him go, deliberately ignoring the large needle in Dr. Simon's hands. Instead, she closed her eyes and sucked in deep calming breaths and pictured being anywhere but there.

~

Tommy hesitated in the doorway of Sadie's bedroom, giving her the space she needed to finish her phone call. He didn't want to intrude, but also didn't want to let her out of his sight.

"I really appreciate it," Sadie said into the phone she'd placed on her lap. "I hate putting so much on you, but I don't want Amelia to see me like this. Not to mention someone has come after me twice now and been in my home. I don't want her in any danger."

"We'll keep her safe." Mrs. Collin's voice rang out from the speaker. "She's excited to stay the night. I've been promising her a sleep over for ages, and Laura will be here tonight as well. She has everything she needs here, and I'll make sure she has a blast. She can stay as long as needed."

Sadie blew out a long, shaky sigh and dashed tears from her eyes. "Thank you. I don't know what I'd do without you."

"We may not be blood, but honey, we're still family. We're here for you. No matter what you need. Now get some rest so this little girl can come home and see her mama."

She smiled. "Can I talk to her?"

A light rustling sounded before Amelia's little voice said, "Hi, Mama! I love you! But I have to go help make popcorn."

"Love you, Baby," Sadie said, smiling.

"All right," Mrs. Collins said. "Go rest now."

Tommy walked to the bed and fluffed another pillow then stuffed it between Sadie's back and the headboard of her bed. "Can I get you anything? Water? Food?"

"What about an ice-cold beer?" Setting her phone on her nightstand, she reached for her computer and settled it on her lap.

He scratched the back of his neck. "I don't think you should have alcohol with the pain medication they prescribed."

She stared at him with hooked eyebrows. "First, I was kidding. Second, I'm only taking over-the-counter pills. I can't afford to let anything affect my thinking."

Tommy dropped onto the mattress. "You mean like a bullet to your head?" Turmoil churned in his gut. As long as he lived, he'd never erase the image of her blood-soaked head, closed eyes, and white face from his mind.

She softened the tight lines around her eyes. "I'm sorry. Today was tough for us both. But we can't stop. Not now. Not when we're so damn close."

He flicked his gaze to the clock then back to her bandaged and battered face. "It's dinner time. Shawn's car's being pored over for evidence. We've put in calls to all the local hospitals requesting records from the month in question. Now it's time to give it a rest. At least for the night. We can hit it hard in the morning. If you're feeling up to it."

She scowled. "I'm fine. I don't need to rest now. I want to search for articles for deaths or injuries caused by a car for the month the storage unit was first rented."

Licking his lips, he gained a firm grasp on his slipping composure. "We'll have more luck searching their archived newspapers they keep on hand. And even if you found something of interest right now, it won't be much use without the aid of the records we need from the hospitals. Everyone we called was already home for the night. If we wake up early, we'll have plenty of time to read through the newspapers before most of the administrative staff at the hospitals are even at their desks."

Snapping her computer closed, she drooped her shoulders and offered a weary smile. "You're right. And I am getting hungry. But I'll only eat if you let me get out of this ridiculous bed."

"Isn't it supposed to be romantic when a man brings his woman food in bed? On a fancy tray with a flower beside it."

She folder her arms over her chest. "Your woman?"

Suppressing a laugh, he shrugged. They hadn't discussed the status of their relationship, and he didn't have the first clue the right way to bring it up. But one thing was for sure—after today, he had no doubts about the part he wanted her to play in his life. The only uncertainty lay with how Sadie felt.

"And where in the world would you find a random flower in the middle of winter? Not in my house, that's for sure."

Leaning forward, he pressed his lips to hers. If he didn't stop her, she'd go on and on about the flower and the tray and everything else besides the one thing he really wanted to discuss. "Forget the bed. We can eat in the kitchen. I'll order pizza." Not like he was hungry. His unasked questions and the trauma of the day sat heavy in his stomach, but he needed to make sure she ate.

"Sounds perfect."

Helping her to her feet, he kept his gait slow as he guided her into the living room and onto the sofa. Mittens leapt off the windowsill and nestled into a ball on her lap. A loud purr vibrated from his throat.

Sadie ran her fingers over his head. "He always seems to know when I need a little extra love."

"I can help you with that." Tommy settled his arm over her shoulder and pulled her close. "And not just tonight. I want you to know, I—"

Ring, Ring

Sadie shot forward. Pain rippled across her face. She stilled, pressing the tips of her fingers to her temple.

"I'll gab your phone. You stay put."

"Go ahead and answer it. The call could be important."

Cursing the bad timing, Tommy jogged into her room and grabbed the phone from the nightstand. He could have told her to wait, finished what he wanted to say, but her mind would be on who was calling. And if the person on the other end was Amelia, she'd take priority over anything he could say. Better to take the call then talk.

An unknown number flashed across the screen. He

answered the call and pressed the speaker button. "Deputy Pennel's phone."

"Umm, hello. This is Jess Sproles. Deputy Pennel asked me to call. Said it was important."

"Give me one second. I'll grab her." The name quickened his pace back to his spot on the couch beside Sadie. He held the phone so they could both hear the conversation. He mouthed, "It's Jess Sproles."

Sadie widened her eyes. "Hello. This is Deputy Pennel."

"Hi. You said you had some questions for me." Jess's voice was soft and uncertain.

"Yes, thank you so much for calling. I have some questions regarding Shawn Downs." She bit into her bottom lip.

Tommy tightened his grip on the phone. Hopefully Jess didn't spook easy and hang up before Sadie secured the information they needed.

"I dated Shawn years ago, and only for a few months. What could I possibly have to tell you?"

"Shawn Downs was murdered." Sadie kept her tone soft and friendly. Something Tommy hadn't thought possible before he'd been forced to work with her. "My partner and I are trying to put together some missing pieces from his past. We think you could have some of the answers we need."

A beat of silence pulsed through the speaker. "I... wow... that's awful about Shawn. He was such a nice, fun guy when I met him. I haven't talked to him since he dropped out of school and returned home. That seems like a lifetime ago."

Sadie shifted, a small wince taking over her expression.

Tommy switched the phone to his other hand, using the one closest to her to brush a stray piece of hair from her face. "Are you okay?" he whispered.

She nodded as she continued her conversation with Jess. "I know a lot of time has passed, but it's clear something happened to Shawn to make him quit school. I spoke with his roommate, who told me Shawn spent all his free time with you so you might have better insight. Do you know what happened?"

A long sigh came from the other end of the line. "I wish I did. He was upset that his mom was sick and pissed at his dad. That's why he went home so often. He didn't want his mom to be alone and didn't trust his dad to take care of her. It killed him being away."

"Do you think that's why he dropped out and moved home?" Sadie asked.

"I wouldn't know. He went home one weekend, came back for a week, then left. I never talked to him after that."

"Does anything stand out as odd—beyond his decision to leave school?" Her green eyes gleamed with hope.

Jess huffed out a humorless laugh. "The whole thing was bizarre, but his dad brought him back to school. He didn't have his car. Said something happened to it while he was home."

Sadie straightened. "Do you remember when that was? The month or a time frame to work with?"

"Actually, I do. I was pissed because I wanted him to stay at school for one weekend. It was homecoming. I was young and selfish and didn't understand why the guy I was dating couldn't do the normal college festivities with me. We got into a big fight. He left, I participated in the homecoming events with my friends, then he came back to campus an emotional mess and that was the end."

Anticipation brought Tommy to his feet.

Sadie grabbed the phone with a trembling hand. "Thank you so much for your time. You've been a huge help."

Tommy blocked out the rest of her words and pulled out his phone. He searched his browser for the date of the homecoming football game the weekend Shawn was a freshman in college. “Call back the hospitals. We know what dates to look for now. We’re finally going to figure out what the hell happened to Shawn Downs.”

24

Tommy's exhilaration at narrowing down the dates that Shawn might have wrecked his car morphed into dread. He sank back onto the couch, his eyes fixed on his phone's screen. The longer he stared, unblinking, the more the words and letters blurred. Memories of his mother's accident flew in to take their place.

A phone call, his panicked father rushing him, Owen and Katherine to the hospital, a funeral days later. His grandfather spiraling into depression. The hit and run had never been solved, leaving him and his family devastated and the rest of the town on edge for years. If Tina Wells could be killed just taking a walk through town, anyone could. Especially with the driver still at large.

He rubbed his aching chest with his free hand.

"Tommy? Are you okay?" Sadie rested a palm on his knee, her tired eyes narrowed as she studied him.

He blinked a few times, chasing away the ugly memories. Raw emotion burned his throat. "I need water."

Jumping to his feet, he hurried into the kitchen. He grabbed a glass from the cabinet and filled it halfway with water from the sink. He gulped the cool liquid, letting the drink wash down the suffocating sadness.

His mind raced as he ran through the details of the case. Was it more than a coincidence that Shawn crashed his car the same weekend his mom was killed in a hit and run?

No. It wasn't possible. He was tired and his body was pumped full of every feeling under the sun after what he'd been through the last few days. He finished his water and set the empty glass on the counter, leaning his back against the smooth granite.

Sadie shuffled into the kitchen, a grimace on her face as she took a seat at the four-person farmhouse table. "Is everything all right?"

Guilt took up residence in his chest. She didn't need to follow him around the house, worrying. He pulled up a chair in front of her and sat. Her knees bumped against his. Leaning forward, he grazed the sides of her legs with his knuckles. "The dates of the homecoming from the year Shawn was a freshman were the same weekend as my mom's accident. So he hit something and smashed up his car the same weekend someone hit my mom and left her for dead."

"Wow." She slipped her hands over his. "That's a hell of a coincidence."

"Right. A coincidence." He nodded along with the words. "That's all it can be. I mean, it's crazy to think Shawn Downs had anything to do with my mom's death."

But what if they were missing something? What if after all these years, he could finally get some closure over what happened to his mom?

"Nothing is crazy. This case has had us all over the place, nothing is quite what it seems." She gave his hands a gentle squeeze. "Linking the dates is natural. And it's something we should keep in mind. But like you told me earlier, we need hospital records before we can make any concrete connections."

He rose and rubbed at his temples, pacing across the tile floor. "You're right. We need those records. I don't think I can wait until morning."

"I can ask Jenna Simon to take a look. She's been volunteering at the shelter, and we've connected a bit. She might be willing to help."

"Good idea. You call and get that pizza." He palmed his phone. "I should talk to Owen and Katherine. And my dad. He'd know what evidence they still have. We should send it in to see if any fabrics or DNA were found on the car that match the crime scene from my mom."

Sadie shook her head. "Let's not get them involved until we have more details. I'm sure the hospitals will provide multiple injuries that could relate to Shawn's accident. Even if Shawn had something to do with your mom's accident, it doesn't make sense that he was murdered."

"You're right." His insides shook as the idea took hold in his mind.

"Let me call Jenna."

He hung his head. Questions spun in circles in his mind until he thought he might explode.

She scrolled through her contact list and pressed the speaker button. She eyed him with raised brows. "We both listen. Only I talk. Deal?"

He wanted to smile, but he couldn't make his face cooperate. Not when years of unanswered questions and a flood of emotions held him down. "Deal."

A few seconds passed before the line picked up. "Hey, Sadie. Is everything okay?" Jenna's cheerful voice chirped through the line.

"Not really. I need a favor. Tommy and I have calls in to all the hospitals in the tri-county area. We need records from years ago of all emergency room cases consistent with injuries from a car accident." She kept her gaze on Tommy as she spoke.

His stomach churned.

"As in the victim was involved in a car crash?" Jenna asked.

"Yes, or even hit by a car."

Tommy closed his eyes and tightened his muscles as her words hit him like a boxer's right hook.

"Okay. It might take a while to get those files. Especially since the administrative staff won't be in until the morning."

"I understand, but this is urgent. It's related to the Downs case. If there's any way for you to use some pull to get answers tonight, we'd really appreciate it."

"I'll try, but I can't make any promises. What are the dates?" Wariness slowed Jenna's words.

Sadie gave her the dates, and Tommy tried to steady the rapid rhythm of his heart. "You can call me or Tommy with any information."

"I'll see what I can do."

Jenna clicked off the line and bile sloshed in Tommy's stomach. Sadie'd been right. This case had taken so many twists and turns, and the latest one might lead him straight to his mother's killer.

THREE-QUARTERS OF A PIZZA Tommy had ordered stared up at Sadie from the coffee table. The television blared in the background, but she had no clue what was playing. Her mind spun in a million different directions, each time landing directly on Tommy's mom. So many different parts of their investigation pointed toward something bigger happening around them.

Could the hit and run that had killed Mrs. Wells really be at the center of it all?

Yes, the murder of a Water's Edge resident was a big deal. But nothing had been cut and dry about the entire case. Someone had come after her and Tommy, a break-in at her home resulted in the cold case files being stolen, and another murder had been committed as a set-up to blame Shawn's death on the wrong person.

Someone in town had a secret, and they'd do anything to keep it buried.

Tommy sat beside her. He'd laid his half-eaten piece of pizza beside the open box. His phone rested on his lap. His gaze dropped to the screen every few minutes.

"Staring at your phone won't make it ring, ya know. Jenna said she probably wouldn't get any information tonight." Her heart ached for Tommy. He hadn't stopped fidgeting with anything near him—the blanket draped over the back of the couch, a loose thread on the throw pillow beside him, rubbing the pad of his thumb on the top of his thigh over and over again—since they'd sat to pick at the pizza neither of them really wanted.

He sighed. "I just can't stop thinking about it. All this energy is zipping around my body, demanding I spring into action, and there's not a damn thing I can do."

She pushed her hair behind her ear, wincing when her fingers brushed against the tender spot where the stitches held her skin together. "We need to talk to Melissa Downs in the morning. See if she has any information about what happened to Shawn's car. He would have gotten in an accident around the time they started spending time together."

Tommy hooked an arm on the back of the couch, his fingers resting on her shoulder. "Agree, and I'd like a solid reason why the two never split. I'm tired of all these damn secrets."

Mittens leapt on the sofa and nestled between them. Sadie

rubbed his favorite spot behind his ears. "The biggest question is what does the car have to do with the murder? It could be completely unrelated. If Shawn did commit some crime, how does that lead to his killer?"

Tommy shrugged. "I don't know."

"Curtis is the most likely one to have had dirt on Shawn," Sadie said, recalling the despicable files the bar owner kept regarding all the gossip he'd uncovered for so many people in town. "But he's dead, and the person who killed Shawn is probably the same person who killed Curtis."

"Could Curtis have told someone what happened?" Tommy grabbed his water from the coffee table and took a large gulp. "And why would they care? Curtis was already blackmailing Shawn. We didn't find any reason to believe anyone else was involved."

"Mitch Parson is still at large. He could be responsible, and the car is just a dead end."

He raised a shoulder. "Who knows. This case has taken us down one path just to make us turn around and find another. The car feels like something, though. I trust my gut. We just need to figure out what it can tell us."

"I trust your gut, too." She smiled and warm, fuzzy bursts of happiness tingled through her. "I trust you." The admission was a huge leap of faith on her part. They hadn't discussed what their physical relationship meant—if they'd try to make a go out of a relationship or not. But damn, she wanted it more than anything. The admission excited and terrified her. Especially since she wasn't sure where Tommy's heart was.

Or how he felt about taking on a package deal. Tommy was great with Amelia, but that didn't mean he wanted to take on a bigger role in her daughter's life. And if he didn't want a bigger role in Amelia's life, he had no place in hers.

He cupped her cheek with his palm. "That means a lot. I know trust doesn't come easy for you."

She waited a beat, wanting to hear more, but he offered nothing else. She fought the sting of disappointment. Besides, she might not know where his heart was but she knew for sure where his head was—circling every detail he remembered about his mom's accident.

"How are you feeling?" He narrowed his eyes, as if he stared hard enough he could make sure she told the truth.

The earlier pounding against her skull had dimmed to a faint ache. "I'm fine. Just tired." Even before they'd left the hospital, fatigue had pulled at her eyelids.

"You should sleep."

She glanced at the clock. "I can't remember the last time I was in bed before 9:00 p.m., but nothing sounds better."

"We'll get a good night's rest and wake up refreshed and ready to tackle everything on your new to-do list." He grinned.

She swatted his chest. "Don't knock the list."

The buzz of a call vibrated the coffee table. Straightening, Tommy swiped his phone and glanced at the screen. He frowned. "It's my dad." He answered and his frown turned into a hard scowl as he listened to the words she strained her ears to hear. "I'll be right there."

All ideas of sleep fled her mind at the serious set of Tommy's mouth. As soon as he disconnected, she pounced. "What's wrong? Where are we going?"

He rose and stuffed his phone in his pocket. "I'm going uptown. You're staying here and going to bed."

She shot to her feet, the quick motion making her head swim. But she couldn't show any sign of weakness. Not if she wanted to go wherever the hell the sheriff wanted them. "Like hell I am. I go where you go."

"Not after the day you had. A freaking bullet—"

She held up her hand and gave him her best don't-say-another-word scowl—the one that always worked when Amelia tried to nag her into a new toy at the store. "I know what happened today. I'm fine. Now tell me. What happened?"

"Someone set fire to Town Tavern. The place was full, and everything is crazy. All hands on deck."

She mentally blocked out all the pain and fatigue. Another act of arson. Whoever was terrorizing this town was escalating, and she wouldn't let anything get in her way of putting a stop to it.

25

Red and blue lights slashed across the clear night sky. Flames waved wildly from the top of Town Tavern. Firetrucks clogged the street, police cruisers and ambulances scattered around. Tommy parked as close as he could get to the bar. Citizens milled about, mouths open and eyes wide as they watched the inferno burn through the historic brick building.

He switched off the engine and turned toward Sadie. "You can stay in the car if you aren't feeling up to dealing with this. No one would give it a second thought."

Everyone at the station had learned of Sadie's injury. A night off—even in the midst of an extreme act of arson—was more than acceptable. Not to mention it would lessen his concern over her wellbeing, leaving him to focus entirely on helping with the injured patrons and complete chaos in front of them.

"I told you. I'm fine." She pushed out the passenger door.

Frustration pulsed against his neck. If she wanted to be stubborn, so be it. He jogged to her side, and stuck close as they dodged through the crowded sidewalk. Thick smoke bloomed around the singed bar.

Firemen with large hoses aimed streams of water on the flames. Paramedics escorted coughing men and women to waiting ambulances to check their vitals. A booming voice caught Tommy's attention. "There's my dad."

Sadie increased her pace to keep up with him.

Mike frowned in her direction. "You should be home, Deputy Pennel."

She pulled back her shoulders. "You told Deputy Wells all hands on deck. I'm here, and I want to help."

Mike's frown stayed in place. "Fine. But you are to sit in an ambulance and take statements while people are being looked at."

"But I—"

"No arguments. I want you off your feet as much as possible. I won't have one of my deputies falling over from exhaustion because they're too stubborn to know their limits."

Tommy wouldn't dare say it out loud, but he agreed with his dad and applauded his hard-nosed response to Sadie being on the scene.

"Tommy," Mike said, cutting into his thoughts. "I want you to talk to the Fire Marshal and the first deputies on scene. Whoever started this fire waited until the place was packed."

Tommy nodded.

"Get to work." Mike hurried over to a group of first responders.

"I guess I'll see you in a bit." Sadie pursed her lips.

He cupped her shoulder with his hand. "I'll let you know if I find anything. I promise. Go take care of people. They need help, and keeping people safe is the most important part of our job."

A tiny grin peeked through her pissed-off pout. "I can't argue when you put it like that."

He wiggled his eyebrows. "I know. Now go."

Turning, he hurried over to a cluster of deputies taking statements. He focused on the woman beside Deputy Grant. "How's everyone doing?"

The woman shivered, even with a blanket wrapped around her shoulders. Soot stained her cheeks, her eyes widened with disbelief. "I've never been so scared in my life."

Anger burned the pit of his stomach. "I'm sorry, ma'am. Must have been awful." He flicked his glance to the older deputy scribbling in a notepad. "Were you first on scene?"

He nodded. "One of them. Not sure what caused the fire yet. Fire Marshal hasn't confirmed anything."

Tommy's phone vibrated against his thigh. Anticipation tightened his chest. It could be Dr. Simon. He grabbed his phone, and the name on the screen had him beating back frustration. An unknown number.

Taking a deep breath of smoky air, he answered the call. "Deputy Wells."

"It's Melissa Downs. We need to talk."

He tightened his jaw. He wanted to talk to Judge Downs, but not now. Even if a million questions burned the tip of his tongue. "Things are a bit hectic right now. How about we talk in the morning?"

"It's important."

"And it can't wait?" Tommy blew out a breath and took in the scene. Yes, he needed to take statements, but his main objective was to figure out what happened to Shawn. If talking to Melissa could help him do that, he should take a minute to see what she had to say.

"I have stuff to show you. Things Shawn buried behind his house."

Tommy scratched the whiskers along his jawline. He hadn't thought to dig through the frozen ground to search for evidence. What would Shawn go through that much trouble to hide? Indecision bounced inside him.

"Please." Melissa softened her tone, her voice cracking. "What I found could help find his killer."

The cracking of her voice melted any resolve Tommy possessed. That and a building need to find out once and for all what happened—and if it involved his mom. Melissa could be the only one who had those answers. "Fine. I'll be there soon."

"Thank you. I can't fix the relationship I screwed up with my husband, but if I can help seek justice, it might ease a fraction of the guilt that's eaten me up inside for so long."

Tommy glanced around and hurried toward his vehicle. Things were under control for the most part, and he could always read through statements taken by the other deputies. He shot Sadie a quick text letting her know he was heading to Shawn's and would be back soon. She didn't need to be running around all over town. Staying here, where medics could keep an eye on her, was for the best.

He quickened his pace against the harsh wind. If he was lucky, he'd be back on the scene of the fire before Sadie found out he was gone. If not, he had no doubt she'd let him have it. A smile cracked through the somber set of his mouth. She was a firecracker. One he wanted to handle for a long time to come.

A CHILL SETTLED deep within Sadie's bones. Heat pumped from the vents of the ambulance she sat in, but the open back doors made it impossible to stay warm. The handful of people who'd stood outside, waiting for vitals to be taken and reassurances, had scattered—statements given.

She jumped down from the ambulance on a huff of irritation. The emergency medics didn't even look her way as she hurried into the thinning crowd in search of Tommy.

Her phone vibrated in her pocket, and she pulled it out.

Jenna.

Her heart lodged in her throat. "Hi, Jenna. Did you find something?" She continued down the sidewalk, checking faces in the dim streetlights for Tommy.

"Hi, Sadie. I tried calling Tommy, but he didn't answer."

Unease pricked the back of her neck. Tommy had practically watched his screen all evening waiting for Jenna to call. She ignored the sensation. She was being silly. There was a lot going on, and Tommy was probably busy taking statements, trying to figure out who started the fire. "Things are pretty crazy right now. Not sure if you've heard. There was a fire at Town Tavern. He's probably busy talking to witnesses."

"I heard about the fire after I came into the hospital to check the files for you guys." Exhaustion made her words come out slow.

She stilled, lowering her head and plugging a finger in her ear to hear every word over the commotion. "What did you find?"

"The weekend you asked about, there were only a couple of injuries consistent with a car accident. A couple teenagers hit a deer and had some minor injuries that were treated in the emergency room and released that Friday. The following afternoon a man ran into a tree—broken arm and concussion. Again, nothing with an unknown cause of injury."

She nodded along with the words. "Okay. Anything else?"

"Then there's Tina Wells."

A fist of apprehension squeezed her chest. "She's the only victim of a car-related incident who was treated at the hospital that weekend with no idea what happened?"

"Yes. I mean, it's a county hospital but it's still small. Not a lot of activity. You mentioned you had calls into other the county hospitals. They might have more unexplained incidents."

The pain that had ebbed in her head came back with a vengeance, along with a swirl of bile in her stomach. Jenna was right. The other hospitals might have more incidents to investigate. But instinct screamed she had the information she needed. Besides, if Shawn came home every weekend to spend time with his mom, why would he have gone anywhere else to joy ride? "Thanks, Jenna."

She disconnected and rushed ahead.

Deputy Grant caught her attention. He stood at the corner, eyes glazed as he watched the dying fire. He lifted a palm in greeting as she approached.

"Have you seen Deputy Wells?" she asked, skipping any pleasantries.

"For a minute earlier." Fatigue hunched his shoulders. "What a night. I've never seen anything like this before. Whoever started this fire is complete scum."

"Agreed. But any idea where Tommy went? I need to find him. Now."

"He left."

"What?" Anger surged to life inside her, chasing away the aches and pains. "Where did he go?"

Deputy Grant shrugged. "Don't know. I was too busy working to listen to his phone conversation. Looked serious, though."

She grunted out her frustration and checked her phone for any texts or calls she may have missed.

No freaking way. Tommy went to Shawn's trailer to talk to Melissa without her. He must have sent her a message when she'd been knee-deep in taking statements, too busy to notice. She pulled up his number and pressed send.

No answer.

"I need you to drive me. Tommy just went off alone, and I don't have my car."

She sent off a text to Tommy and followed Deputy Grant to his cruiser. How could he leave her behind on something so important? She just hoped she could keep her temper in check when she found Tommy. Water's Edge didn't need another dead body to add to the count.

26

Tommy parked next to Melissa's car in the gravel drive in front of Shawn's trailer. He stepped out into the brutal cold and zipped up his jacket. The yellow crime scene tape in front of Shawn's door hung loose, the end whipping in the breeze.

Melissa exited her car and met him by the front door.

Tension wound a tight ring around Tommy's neck. The night was quiet, the only light this far in the woods the muted moon beams that penetrated the thicket of trees.

"Thanks for coming," Melissa said. "I can't begin to explain the myriad of emotions I've gone through since Shawn's murder. It's made me examine a lot of the mistakes I've made in my life. Something that's not easy."

Tommy tipped up the corners of his mouth in what he hoped passed as an understanding look. "I'm sure it's been very difficult."

He followed Melissa inside the trailer, now filled with the scents of the crime scene unit as well as the underlaying stench of garbage.

"Do you have any more leads?" Melissa asked as she moved into the dingy living room.

"Same as before." Tommy didn't want to divulge too much information.

"I see. Any clue where Mitch Parson is?"

"No, ma'am."

"Well, you might want to increase the intensity of your search when you see what I found. I put the box on the kitchen table." Melissa flicked her glance toward the tiny space beside them. "I should warn you. What I found is a bit disturbing."

Tommy raised his brows. The warning was unnecessary. Nothing could be more disturbing than seeing Shawn's bullet-pierced body lying in the middle of a meadow. But he'd keep that thought to himself. "Whatever it is, I appreciate you bringing it to my attention."

Melissa sighed. "Let's get this over with."

Tommy crossed the stained linoleum floor of the kitchen. A small, dirt-caked box sat on the fold-out table that jutted from the wall. He lifted the top and set it aside.

"I still can't believe what I read. Or that Shawn would be involved in something so scandalous. His entire life could have turned out so much differently."

Tommy glanced over his shoulder. Melissa had taken a step closer and peered down at the box.

Anticipation tickled Tommy's fingertips as he dug inside. This could finally be what he and Sadie had been searching for. The key that would unlock all the secrets and tell him exactly what had happened to Shawn and why.

He rummaged through a pile of loose papers. More drawings and cryptic messages like the ones he'd found hidden in the siding of Shawn's trailer littered the table, but nothing that filled in all the missing blanks of the case.

"I'm not seeing what you're so upset about." He grabbed a

handful of papers and flipped through them. "Can you show me what you found that was so important?"

Footsteps fell behind him. Melissa's proximity put him on alert. A warning rang in his brain. Something wasn't right.

Turning, he came face to face with Melissa Downs. A knife in her hand. Pointed directly at Tommy's chest.

Tommy raised his hands, mentally cursing all the mistakes he'd made by coming here alone, with only a stupid text to Sadie about where he'd gone. No telling how long it would take her to see it. "What's going on, Judge?"

"You know too much, and I won't let you ruin everything I worked so damn hard for. I already got rid of Curtis, now it's time for you to go bye-bye, too."

If Tommy was going to figure a way out of this, he had to keep Melissa talking. "So, you were covering for Shawn all this time? Is that why you two stayed married? Some weird arrangement where he paid for your silence?"

Melissa laughed, the sound loud and menacing. "Maybe you aren't as smart as I thought. But it doesn't matter now."

Tommy crinkled his brow, trying to make sense of Melissa's words. "I don't understand. If Shawn didn't commit a crime with his car, what happened?"

The judge stopped laughing, an amused smirk hitching up one side of her mouth. "Maybe it's fair you finally find out what happened to your mom before you die."

"What?" His heart fell to the floor. "Shawn killed my mom?"

"No, you idiot. I did."

Anger surged through Tommy, and he leapt forward.

The knife jammed into his side. Pain rippled up his torso, and blood poured from the wound. He fell to the ground, Melissa crushed under him. He rolled to his side, but adrenaline and rage kept him alert. He circled his palm around Melissa's wrist and slammed it against the floor.

Melissa dropped the knife. She scrambled to her knees and surged forward, trying to reclaim her grip on the handle.

Tommy stretched for the weapon, his side screaming in protest.

Melissa kicked Tommy where the knife had pierced his skin.

Stars erupted behind his closed eyes. Agony shot through him. He curled into a ball, grabbing his side.

The cold tip of a blade pressed against his throat. He opened his eyes and stared up into the cold, dark eyes of the woman who planned to kill him.

Another swift kick and his world went black.

SADIE POUNDED her fist against Shawn's thin door. She tapped the toe of her booted foot against the concrete stoop, training her ears for any movement inside the house.

A loud *thud* sounded and the tiny structure shook.

Adrenaline shot through her veins. "What was that?"

A deep frown pulled at Deputy Grant's bulldog-mouth. "Sounds like something heavy fell or a fight breaking loose."

"We need to get inside. Now."

She secured her gun in her hands, shouldered open the flimsy barrier and swept into the room. All the pain in her head fled.

Melissa Downs crouched low to the ground with a knife in her hand, the blade pressed against Tommy's neck. Blood seeped onto the floor.

She trained her gun at Melissa's head. "Freeze. Put your hands in the air. You're under arrest."

Deputy Grant stood beside her, feet planted wide, his weapon also aimed at Melissa.

Melissa cocked her head to the side and smiled. She kept

the pointed tip of her weapon against Tommy. "Deputy Pennel. What an interesting surprise. And convenient, too. I can take care of you both right now. How lucky for me. But too bad for Deputy Grant. Wrong place at the wrong time I guess."

She fought not to drop her gaze to Tommy's motionless form. She had to keep all her focus on Melissa. "Do you think I'd just let you stab me? You have two guns aimed directly on you. You have no escape. No need to make this harder than necessary. Drop your weapon. Lift your hands."

She took a step forward.

Melissa clicked her tongue. She pressed the knife harder against Tommy's skin. "Not so fast. You might get off a shot, but not before I plunge this knife into Tommy. Are you willing to risk that? Especially with your...special relationship?"

"You're full of shit. Now drop the knife." How would she know anything about her relationship with Tommy? Hell, she didn't even know if they *were* in a relationship, but whatever was between them, she'd been careful to keep it under wraps as much as possible.

Melissa laughed. "Don't like that I know so much about you, do you, Deputy?"

She studied the wicked gleam in the judge's eyes. "You've followed us. Trying to kill us both, breaking into my house to steal Tina Wells' files, and starting the fire at the bar. You needed to draw us out, separate us, to get to Tommy."

Melissa grinned. "I'd applaud your brilliance at putting things together, but my hands are full."

"Did Shawn hit Tina Wells and leave her to die?" Sadie tried to pull together all the information they'd collected to form a full picture, but something still didn't make sense. "No. You wouldn't lie for years and stay married to a man like Shawn to protect him. Not to mention there'd be no reason to keep protecting Shawn now that he's dead. If his secret came out, who cares? It doesn't hurt you or anyone else at this point."

Melissa worked her jaw back and forth.

She'd hit a nerve. She needed to push harder. "And why would anyone else kill Shawn as revenge for what he'd done?"

A tiny vein bulged at Melissa's temple. "Enough."

"You told me you two started spending time together when he came home on weekends. That you rushed into a marriage, even though he'd had a girlfriend back at college weeks before. And you've stayed married to the town alcoholic, even though he was sleeping with someone else, and nobody can understand why."

Everything snapped into place—the car, the storage unit, the cryptic messages left behind by Shawn. "Unless Shawn wasn't alone when he ran into Tina Wells."

"I said enough! Shut up!" Red flooded Melissa's cheeks.

Disgust coated her stomach as the truth smacked her in the face. "You had to keep Shawn quiet, too, didn't you? Was the guilt too much for him? Was he finally going to spill your secret?"

"Your time is up. Say goodbye to your boyfriend." Melissa dropped her gaze to the knife digging into Tommy's neck. Blood seeped from beneath the blade.

Sadie aimed the gun at Melissa's knee and pulled the trigger.

"You bitch!" Melissa collapsed into a screaming pile on the ground.

Sadie ran forward and kicked the dropped knife out of her reach.

Deputy Grant secured Melissa's hands behind her back with handcuffs.

Sadie fell to her knees at Tommy's side. "Call an ambulance." Fear made her words tremble more than her erratically pounding heart. She couldn't lose Tommy. Not after it took her so damn long to find him.

She scanned his blood-soaked shirt. With gentle fingers she

lifted the stiff material of his brown uniform. Red stained his torso. Sweat dotted her hairline, and her hands shook. Panic and fear mingled into a giant ball of lead in her throat.

"Ambulance will be here soon," Deputy Grant said.

A soft moan had her shifting her attention to Tommy's face. His hooded eyes and pale pallor spiked her blood pressure. He needed help. Fast.

"Sadie."

She leaned down to hear him and applied pressure to the wound. Blood covered her hands, the irony smell making her dizzy and threatening to pull her back into the past.

But she had to stay present, be in the moment to help Tommy however she could. "Help's on the way. Everything's fine. Just relax." Pressure built in her sinus cavity, and she blinked back tears. She couldn't fall apart. Not when Tommy needed her most.

"She killed my mom. She was driving the car. Not Shawn." His eyelids slipped closed.

She waited for them to open, to tell him that he'd finally gotten justice for his mom, but his eyes stayed shut as the wailing of the siren came closer. And when the paramedics burst through the door, all she could do was watch in horror as they pushed her away and worked to save the life of the man she loved.

27

Tommy closed his eyes and sucked in a deep breath of cold air before standing on weak legs. Being in the hospital overnight had made the stringent scent of disinfectant take up permanent residence in his nostrils.

But he couldn't complain. Things would have been a lot worse if Sadie hadn't shown up when she did. The paramedics had stopped the bleeding on the way to the hospital, and Dr. Simon's steady hand had stitched his side back together. He was one lucky sonofabitch that no internal organs had been nicked.

"Sit down," Sadie said.

"There's no reason for you to wheel me to the stupid car. Hospital policy is I have to be pushed out the door in a wheelchair. Once I'm outside, I'm a free man." He sneezed. The stitches on his side stretched. He doubled over and held his ribs until the pain subsided. "Damn. Sneezing hurts almost as bad as being stabbed."

"Not so tough now, free man. Now sit." Sadie pushed down on his shoulders until he relented then moved slowly across the parking lot to her car. "And comparing a stab wound to a sneeze might be the most ridiculous thing I've ever heard. But if it hurts that bad, I should take you home. When the doctor discharged you this morning, he said you needed rest."

"I agreed to that before I found out Melissa Downs was being questioned at the station. I need to be there." A fresh wave of anger washed over him. He clenched his fists on his lap. All these years, the people responsible for ripping away his mom had been right under his nose, living their lives as though nothing had happened.

At least Shawn had succumbed to guilt, or that's what Tommy assumed led him down a path of alcoholism. But Melissa had kept moving up the ranks, not letting anything slow her down until she got where she wanted.

"I understand. I'd want to be there if I were you." Sadie rolled him as close as possible to the passenger side door and helped him to his feet after opening it. "But after, we both deserve some time off."

Leaning an arm on the top of the door, he cupped her cheek. Little marks dinged her face and black stiches ran along her temple. "How about a vacation? You, me, and Amelia. Time where we can talk about what we really want out of life—from each other." He still hadn't found an opportunity to dive into a deep conversation about where things stood between them, but he would.

She grinned. "I'd like that, but are you sure you can handle that much time with a rambunctious six-year-old?"

"Absolutely." A knot of tension loosened at the back of his neck. Screw it. He didn't need a perfect time to tell her how he felt. If the past days taught him anything, it was that life was short. "But just so you know. I want you, Sadie. Every part of you. I want to make this work because I think we're great together."

A light blush stained her cheeks. She pressed her lips to his. "I think so, too."

Happiness tightened his chest. The next couple of hours would be tough, but at least he'd have Sadie by his side. He climbed in the car and took her hand after she returned the wheelchair and buckled into the driver's seat. Silence settled between them, his mind fixed on what was to come. By the time she pulled into her spot behind the station, his nerves were as taut as a tightrope.

She shut off the engine. "Ready?"

He sucked in a shuddering breath. "As I'm ever going to be."

They walked hand-in-hand into the station, neither giving a damn who saw them or what they thought. Melissa sat in the interview room, a cast covering her leg where Sadie had shot her.

Tommy led Sadie to the room beside it where he could watch the police chief of Water's Edge, Chief Buckman, squeeze whatever he could out of the disgraced judge. The gun used to shoot Shawn and Sadie had been found in Melissa's house, so she'd go to prison no matter what she divulged. But the need to find out exactly what happened to his mom beat a constant rhythm in his heart.

Katherine, Theo, Owen, Marie, and his dad shot to their feet the moment he stepped across the threshold. Pappy sat in the corner, arms crossed. Tears streamed down Katherine's face. She rushed toward him and threw her arms around his neck.

He kept one hand locked with Sadie's and secured his free arm around Katherine's back.

"I can't believe it." Katherine kept her face pressed against him as she spoke. "After all these years, we find out who killed her."

His dad approached and rested a heavy hand on his shoulder. "Good work, Son. Your mother would be proud." His words came out thick, as if his throat would close at any moment.

Tears misted his eyes, and he pressed his lips together until the pale pink turned white. "I'm proud."

Owen sniffed back emotion and gave one brief nod, no words needed to be spoken to understand the depth of his feelings.

"Let's sit. You shouldn't be on your feet." Marie gestured toward the line of chairs in front of the two-way mirror.

Tommy fell into the cushioned seat. His dad sat beside him, then Katherine with Theo on her other side. Marie crossed to sit beside Pappy while Owen stayed on his feet behind her.

"I should step outside," Sadie said. "You need to be with your family. I'll wait for you."

"No way." He pulled her onto the empty chair to his right. "You've been beside me from the start of this, and I want you by my side all the way to the end."

"Are you sure?"

"Yes," Katherine said. "Please, stay."

Sadie nodded and linked her fingers with Tommy's.

Tommy licked his dry lips and faced forward, latching his gaze to the back of Melissa Downs' head. Her lawyer sat beside her. Chief Buckman entered the room and took a seat across from her at the long rectangular table, and the interview began.

As the interview progressed, anger mingled with sorrow. Listening to the woman who killed his mother tell the story of fighting with Shawn while she drove his car, distracted and furious because she wanted him to dump his girlfriend back at college, made his skin crawl.

Tommy had always known his mom had been in the wrong place at the wrong time. But he'd never imagined a stupid argument between Melissa and Shawn had caused the driver—Melissa—to jump the curb, hit his mother, and speed away.

Revulsion churned his stomach, but he couldn't look away—had to hear every detail. Even an estranged wife explaining how her husband's desperation to confess led to shoot and kill a man she'd once loved.

By the time the interview was finished and Melissa was wheeled out in handcuffs, every nerve in Tommy's body shook. "Melissa Downs is a monster."

Mike stood and faced him. Katherine rose and cuddled against her father's side. Owen squeezed Marie's shoulder as she wrapped an arm around Pappy's thin shoulder.

"You're right," Mike said. "And she'll spend the rest of her life in prison to pay for what she's done."

"It won't bring Mom back," Tommy whispered, unable to stop the moisture from pooling in his eyes.

Sadie squeezed his hand. "Nothing will. But you'll keep her alive with your memories and stories. And now, knowing the person responsible for her death is being punished, you can heal. Not completely, but enough so that you can think of your mom with a smile and joy instead of only rage and questions."

She was right. The pain of losing his mom would never go away, but a new sense of peace—of justice—had already begun to grow within him. The path to finding Shawn's killer had taken him in a direction he never expected, but it had given him answers he'd longed to have for so many years.

And had given him Sadie.

EPILOGUE

Sadie stepped into her living room and smiled at the cluttered mess that would have driven her crazy three months earlier. But not now. Now, the mess meant Tommy—the man she loved—was home and waiting for her.

"Tommy? Amelia?" She picked up a jacket from the floor and hung it in the closet before moving further into the home she now shared with the most wonderful man she'd ever met.

"Back here." His strong voice came from the kitchen.

Resisting the urge to clean as she went, she made a beeline to the kitchen, the savory smells of garlic and oregano urging her forward. The table was set with two plates filled with spaghetti and meatballs, two glasses of wine, and a single candle in the middle.

"Mommy! You're home!" Amelia's little voice reached her seconds before her daughter catapulted herself into her arms.

Sadie hugged her tight and kissed the top of her head. She focused on the sweet display in her kitchen and the two people she loved more than anything and not the sauce-splattered stove and dishes piled in the sink. "What did you do?"

Tommy grinned and pulled a chair out for her to sit. "We cooked."

She laughed and hobbled across the room with Amelia still attached and placed a kiss on his cheek before sitting.

Amelia skipped over to Tommy and sat on his lap.

"I see that. Why?" Tommy had a long list of positive qualities, most of them surrounding his total commitment and devotion to her and Amelia, but preparing meals wasn't one of them. Which was fine with her since cooking was something she loved.

He shrugged and circled his arms around Amelia. "Wanted to be nice. Between work and helping at the women's shelter, you've been so busy. We thought you deserved to be pampered a little bit, didn't we goose?"

Amelia giggled at her new nickname.

Warmth spread all the way down to Sadie's toes. She picked up the wine glass and took a sip of the dry red wine. "Pampered is nice."

He pulled out his phone and showed her the screen displaying a grand resort nestled along a beautiful coastline. "That's not all I have. We never took that vacation. What do you think about escaping this nasty March weather and heading to the beach? Warm weather, sandy beaches, and maybe a sitter to help with the rugrat when we need some alone time." A wicked gleam lit his eyes.

She grinned. "Sounds like heaven. When do we leave?" Mentally rolling through her to-do list, she tried to think of the best time to take some days off for a much-needed escape.

"Next week."

She dropped her jaw and set down her glass. "What? That's too soon. I don't even know if I can take the time. I have things to get done before jetting to the beach. And Amelia has school."

"I already talked to the sheriff, who agreed we both deserved a week away. Laura has plenty of help at the shelter and Mrs. Collins said she needs a break so she can come with us. Amelia's teacher said she can give her all the work she'd need to do while we're gone. And there's only one thing on that to-do list of yours that needs handled before we can go."

"I don't have a list right now," she said, hiding her grin behind a smirk.

Amelia jumped off Tommy's lap and grabbed a crumpled sheet of paper from her pocket. "We made you one."

Sadie took the note and read the list the two troublemakers had made. Each line listed the tasks Tommy had already seen to with a check mark beside all but the last sentence, which read *Get final answer.*

He slid a ring box from his pocket and dropped to one knee. "Marry me."

She gasped and pressed her hands to her mouth. "Are you serious?"

Amelia hopped up and down on her toes and clapped her hands. "Say yes! Please, Mommy. Tommy wants to marry us! He wants to be my daddy."

Tommy winked at Amelia then smiled up at Sadie, dimples flashing. "I wouldn't put it on the list if I didn't mean it. And Amelia's right. I love you both more than anything in the world. I want to be her daddy. I want to be your husband. I want us to be a family. Forever. If you'll have me."

She'd never dreamed she could have the kind of happiness Tommy brought into her life. A lifetime with him was more than she'd dared to hope.

Tears filled her eyes, and she dropped her shaking hands. "Yes."

A whoop of joy erupted from his mouth. He sprang to his feet and scooped her and Amelia up against him. She laughed and framed his face with her hands. How had she gotten so damn lucky to find this man? A man filled with joy and kindness and passion. A man who loved her for exactly who she was—who loved her daughter as his own. "I love you, Tommy Wells. I can't wait to be your wife."

DON'T MISS out on Jenna's Threatened Sanctuary, the exciting second chance romance that brings danger and emotion in the fourth book of the Safe Haven Women's Shelter series.

ACKNOWLEDGMENTS

First and foremost, thank you to my husband, Scott. You are always my biggest supporter and that means the world to me. Thanks to my children, Abigail and Vaughn. I couldn't love you more.

Thank you to my fabulous critique partners, Samantha Wilde and Julie Anne Lindsey. Not only do you make my words make sense but you keep me sane on the daily. Your friendship is everything.

To my editor, The Editing Soprano, I appreciate not only all your hard work in making my books shine, but your limitless kindness. And to the Deranged Doctors, thank you for always providing the best covers!

To my readers, you are the reason I get to keep doing what I love. Thank you for reading my books!

Danielle

ABOUT THE AUTHOR

Danielle M Haas is a stay-at-home mom turned author. When she isn't writing fast-paced romantic suspense novels with mysteries to live for and romance to die for, she's busy being a taxi driver to her two busy kids and forcing her introverted self to talk to other soccer moms. Her kids and husband are her world, which is also shared with her hyper Bernie doodle, mini Whoodle, and two sassy cats. Her days are packed with cuddles, kisses, and a brain constantly thinking of new ways to create danger and romance for her next book.

Sign up for Danielle's NEWSLETTER to stay up to date with everything she has going on.

ALSO BY DANIELLE HAAS

Safe Haven Women's Shelter

Laura's Safe Haven

Marie's Hidden Refuge

Injured Heroes Series

Crossroads of Revival

Crossroads of Revenge

Crossroads of Delusion

Crossroads of Redemption

Crossroads of Obsession

Crossroads of Betrayal

Crossroads of Innocence

Code Name: Gemini (A Zodiac Tactical/Injured Heroes Crossover)

Murders of Convenience

Matched with Murder

Booked to Kill

Driven to Kill

The Sheffield's Series

Second Time Around

A Place In This World

Coming Home

Stand Alones

Bound by Danger

Girl Long Gone

www.ingramcontent.com/pod-product-compliance
Lightning Source LLC
LaVergne TN
LVHW100524110826
845146LV00002B/772

* 9 7 9 8 9 8 6 3 9 5 0 8 1 *